"Go on, tell me then, about the sale."

I could see that Marc was getting excited. He'd finished his beer and was moving the empty can around in his hands, denting it as he released the pressure that was building inside himself.

"The entire process is very formal, of course. We went in and those who were to be sold were on display. The servants brought the trays of food and drink into the room and the party proceeded as it had in the foyer.

"Though, of course, now we could do our investigation of the slaves as well. The first two were each kneeling on top of separate mirrored tables. Their legs were spread far apart and were chained at the ankles to keep them that way. So, when you walked up to where they were, not only were their genitals forced forward by their posture, you could also see the reflections of their undersides on the glass.

"Each one had his wrists shackled to the back of his neck by an intricate gold chain that also produced a collar. They were totally naked. They'd have to be since the customers would all insist on seeing everything of any importance.

"The first male was dark in a Latin way. Italian, I suppose, or perhaps French like yourself." The allusion made Marc squirm...

cover art by F. Ronald Fowler

THE LOVE OF A MASTER

John Preston

Alyson Publications, Inc. • Boston

Also by John Preston:

Classified Affairs
(with Frederick Brandt)
Deadly Lies
Entertainment for a Master
Franny: The Queen of Provincetown
Golden Years
Hot Living
I Once Had a Master
Secret Dangers
Stolen Moments
Sweet Dreams

Published as a trade paperback original
by Alyson Publications,
40 Plympton St., Boston, Mass. 02118.

Distributed in the U.K. by GMP Publishers,
PO Box 247, London, N15 6RW, England.

First U.S. edition: July, 1987

ISBN 0-932870-95-3

To Anne, and all the colors of her many cloaks

A Reawakening

I had begun it all again. My party in San Francisco had been more of a re-entry into the life of harsh and complete sexuality than I had ever expected. It was only supposed to have been a single affair, a gift I could give to my friends, an event to remember.

I had thought that my life in the country had been more than the most recent chapter in my life; I had thought it would be the last. But I was wrong and now I knew it. A life is a series of cycles; there are no endings, only stages that have not yet been succeeded.

There was no reason to be upset by this. It was only a question of being surprised, of becoming aware that I was once more on the road to sexual adventure. How strange, I thought, that it would start all over again. Not, how unfortunate; not, how provident; simply, how strange.

The sight of the naked men and their beautiful bodies at my party, the enjoyment of my guests, the visceral pleasure I received from my role in making it all happen — these things combined and there was no way that I could deny my desire to make them occur again. But even more dramatically, even more intensely, and much more for my own pleasure.

I spent the weeks after the party in San Francisco debating my options, looking around at the men who might be of interest to me, and making my renewed interest known to those people who might understand and who would share the passions I felt.

They were not all sympathetic. I received phone calls and letters that were nothing less than insulting with their implications that my "retirement" from the world of S&M had been a sham, or that my intentions weren't understandable. Those calls came from the people who thought that one had to make a pledge to the world of sexuality that was similar to the most draconian religious vows. I had broken mine by moving to the country, living a relatively quiet life, not maintaining the contacts and not making the appearances that they felt were required.

Those were ridiculous rules and responses. There were other people who were much more understanding. They would call and talk about the pleasures and the learnings that were still to be had. These were people who understood that there are those of us who move in and out of the sexual world with some mobility, but never with a lessening of our dedication.

The people from The Network also contacted me. Of course they did. The conversations were pleasant, almost to the point of being mechanical. But while they were going on, small electric shots were being sent through my body. I wanted to be a part of it again. I was desperate for it. I wasn't about to have my re-entry into the world of sex be something that happened just in chic leather bars or with uncommitted people who would only play occasional games. If I was going to do this all again, then let it be at that level: The Network's.

But perhaps not as a part of The Network. I'd have to think about that.

My passions aren't comfortably contained in other people's constructions. That doesn't mean I don't like them or that I can't appreciate the effort that other people put into their sexual work. Far from it. But there is a need to *create* that is best expressed by me when I am conceiving my own composition.

And so I began my re-entry with travel. Madame, my friend and often companion, made contacts for me that I couldn't establish myself — at least not quickly enough. Certain other friends were more than willing to aid me. They made me welcome in their homes and made introductions to new people to whom I might be of use or who might be useful to me.

The experiences were exhilarating and terrifying. They were creating in me a compulsion that I hadn't expected. But they were undeniable in their attraction and I would never be able to ignore the needs that were rising to the surface.

Telling Stories

"What was your trip like?"

Marc is one of the wonders of my hometown. A strikingly handsome young man of French-Canadian descent, he works in one of the many lumber mills. He has been able to create a sexual life for himself that would astonish most of those in New York or San Francisco who consider themselves to be sexual athletes.

We had met nearly five years ago, when I had first moved to northern New England. There is a network of homosexually active men that is in its own way as rich a federation and as secret a fraternity as The Network. They had spotted me as soon as I'd arrived. Marc — then only nineteen — had been the only one in the group to interest me. He was too young and inexperienced for me to risk any sexual play — at least in the first years. But I'd been rewarded with the opportunity to watch him grow and mature. I could sense a verve in him that was at least as attractive as his tall, firm body and bright eyes. He would come to talk, to read my books, to ask his questions of someone who wasn't about to dismiss him. Young men really want only to be taken seriously.

I hadn't taken him seriously enough. I knew that now. He had actually been the one person up here who I most wanted. I had studied his body during the summer, played with seducing him at parties, sometimes even engaged in plain sex with him on winter nights when it seemed the need had been so strong in both of us that neither could deny it.

What would have attracted him to me if not my peculiar form of sexuality? But I had never explored that with him. True, when we had our vanilla sex, I was the one who would take the lead in all ways. But there had been no attempt to go further. Lately, he'd been seeing another young man. They'd recently moved in together and I thought of them as lovers. But young men seldom know what it means to have a "lover." I had no reason to give their relationship so much respect — did I? There was a part of me that said it was the only ethical thing to do, to support young men when they attempt such things.

But Marc would always be here at the house. He'd take liberties with it, moving around the rooms whenever he wanted and coming by to swim whenever the whim struck. How much of that had been for my benefit and how many signals had I been missing, simply because I insisted on assuming that the men of the mountains weren't part of my sexual world?

Now he was sitting across the front porch of my house with me, a can of cold beer in his hand, his refreshment after a hard day's labor. I looked over at him and only shrugged. "It was fine."

"*Fine!*" He shouted at me. "Come on, stop playing with me. What was it like? I can't believe it actually happened, that it exists, that you went, that—"

"It's all very, very true, Marc."

Like many other people who don't live in the major cities, Marc has no sense of their reality. On one hand, he thinks that he is somehow inadequate, lacking some training or experiences that he assumes everyone — or nearly everyone — in a place like New York does have. That's not true. I'd watched his development. He had already created more of a sexual circus here in New England than the vast majority of people I knew in Manhattan would ever believe. For one thing, he wasn't trapped into the belief that there were rules that had to be followed or that there was only one way that things could be done.

But, then, there was another side to Marc's perceptions. When he came up against something like The Network and could know someone involved in it like myself, the reality there was too surreal, much too extreme for him to ever believe it actually existed.

Not that he wanted to disbelieve. Hardly. The desire was obvious. His deeply tanned face showed all the excitement of a child hearing that his fairy tales might really be true. He was leaning forward on his chair with his elbows on his knees. I could see the firm muscles of his arms. His t-shirt — with its dark sweat stains under his arms and around his belly — couldn't hide the very obvious and tremendously appealing evidence of the rest of his muscles as they pressed against the fabric. I admired his body; my enjoyment of it was greatly enhanced because it was naturally his, earned at hard work and not in an artificial and ridiculously expensive gymnasium.

"Tell me about it. Please."

I sat back and took a sip of my own drink. I put my head back against my chair and looked out at the grand vista I have from my porch. In front of me I could see the tallest of the White Mountains. My house sits high on a hill of its own, separated from the peaks by a broad valley. I have almost complete privacy here. You would have to come two miles up a poorly marked drive to get to my home. That had been one of the attractions of the place when I had bought it.

But my mind wasn't here on the natural wonders and beauties of New England. My mind was exactly where Marc wanted it to be, back in New York and on the weekend I'd just spent there. It had been my first invitation to attend a function of The Network in years. I had accepted. It had been . . . awesome.

"You remember Madame, don't you?" I asked.

"The redhead? The one who's so beautiful? The one who wanted me to let her cane me?"

"Her." I laughed a little bit, remembering when my omnisexual Marc had met the omnisexual Madame — what a limiting word "bisexual" is when dealing with two people like them! She had been charming, as she always is with strangers. (Her dealings with those of us who know her well are often less than that.) He had thought that he was going to be able to have a encounter with a highly sophisticated New York editor/lady. She had in mind a most definite type of tryst and, once he understood her intentions, there had been some misunderstandings and some quick re-evaluations between the two of them. It had all been very amusing.

Marc glowered a bit and took a violent swig of his beer, as though that little action could regain the masculinity he thought he had lost during that one interaction. "So?"

"She went to the party with me."

"Party? You call a slave auction a party?"

"Yes. It was that, at one level. You have to understand, Marc, these functions aren't some kind of coercive things that happen in your pornographic fantasies. This is a highly ritualized and actually ethical undertaking."

"It's a slave auction."

"It was, in fact, a slave auction. It took place in an exquisite penthouse on the Upper East Side. It is that kind of apartment that you read about and see photographs of and, somehow, can't really believe that it exists. But it does. "Madame and I arrived. The dress for us was formal. She had on one of her most stunning gowns. It's a floor length skirt of black velvet with a top that's made of a metallic fabric. It's gold or brass colored, incredibly, almost indecently, suggestive. It drapes over her breasts, clinging to each of them. It comes as close to being shocking as anything else she ever wears.

"We were quite the hit when we arrived. There were a number of people I knew but hadn't seen in many years. The party of people — the customers, if you insist — gathered in the foyer of the penthouse. That was a room actually much larger than any room you ever expect to see in New York apartments. It was incredibly lavish.

"We were served cocktails and there were appetizers that were as delicious as any I'd ever seen. The food and drink were served by four slaves, two men and two women. The host is one of the most wealthy men in the world. You'd know his name if I told you. Everyone in America would. He can afford the luxury.

"The two men were naked except for a piece of white silk that was wrapped around their cock and balls and held in place by a thin white silk thread, something on the lines of a very brief jock strap. The effect was to make them seem more naked than they would have appeared if they had no clothing at all.

"Around each of their necks was a collar. Not made of the black leather that one expects with male slaves, but of another piece of white silk. It was tied in a knot which left a long length of fabric flowing down their backs. Still another piece of white silk was tied around their hair. They were gorgeous in those brief and probably humiliating uniforms. I expect that one of the better and more well known designers had been commissioned to produce them.

"They were extremely well trained. Their bodies were in marvelous shape and you could see that every guest was staring at the bare and inviting nipples.

"The two female slaves were dressed in the same way, essentially. Their breasts were naked, and remarkably firm.

"The four of them carried the trays and delivered drinks to the well dressed crowd."

"You say that as though they were just any waiters..."

"Oh, no, Marc. These were far from that."

"Did you do anything with them?"

"Them? No. Nor did anyone else. They were there and I'm sure their owner would have granted a guest's request for their use, but they had duties to attend to. It would have been very unthoughtful to keep them from their work."

"Didn't they want to run away? Weren't there guards or else chains to keep them there?"

"Of course not. I've told you before, your fantasies of these people who own and are owned have nothing to do with their reality. These are people who've chosen to take their places. Just as those on sale had."

"I don't believe you. I can't believe you."

"That's because you insist on looking at sex and slavery — separately and together — as though they had to involve a contest. Conquest is the only dynamic you accept as possible. These people wouldn't have understood that."

"Go on, tell me then, about the sale."

I could see that Marc was getting excited. He'd finished his beer and was moving the empty can around in his hands, denting it as he released the pressure that was building inside himself.

"At a certain point — actually, at exactly the announced hour — the male slaves went and opened the two large doors that provided an entrance into the living room.

"Madame and I followed the crowd into it. The room was spectacular. Its view of the city..."

"I don't care about the view of the city!" Marc smashed the can. "Tell me about the sale."

"The entire process is very formal, of course. We went in and those who were to be sold were on display. The servants brought the trays of food and drink into the room and the party proceeded as it had in the foyer.

"Though, of course, now we could do our investigation of the slaves as well. There were four of them. The first two were each kneeling on top of separate mirrored tables. Their legs were spread far apart and were chained at the ankles to keep them that way. So, when you walked up to where they were, not only were their genitals forced forward by their posture, you could also see the reflections of their undersides on the glass.

"Each one had his wrists shackled to the back of his neck by an intricate gold chain that also produced a collar. They were totally naked. They'd have to be since the customers would all insist on seeing everything of any importance.

"The first male was dark in a Latin way. Italian, I suppose, or perhaps French like yourself." The allusion made Marc squirm. "He had a fine coat of hair on his chest, prominent and well built pectorals. But the most amazing thing about him seemed to be his testicles. While they weren't in any way outsized, they were the sort that have a great deal of skin on the scrotal sac, so they hang far down. Since his legs were forced apart, they were hanging loosely and not touching any other part of his body.

"Whenever a slave has that kind of noticeable attribute, it becomes the focus of much of the attention he's paid. It seemed that nearly every potential buyer who walked up to him felt a need to test them. They were slapped, tugged, pinched, pulled. He was in tears within minutes. I'm sure he must have been used to it, but, of course, testicles are simply too delicate to ever be built up in a way that would sustain someone when they're being tortured."

"So there was torture going on."

"Marc, listen to me, certainly they were playing with his testicles. But this was an elegant affair, a quiet one. The guests were all in black tie or formal gowns. They were simply testing his reactions. They would, after all, be spending a great deal of money to buy him and they had a right to investigate how he would respond.

"In any event, he seemed not too upset, actually. Yes, there were tears, but he was still able to look directly at the customers and even to smile once when one woman put a delicate and loving hand on his cheek. He was very handsome in the classic way of today's magazine models, I must admit that. A little older than most who are sold, I'd say at least thirty, but the fashion for youth is passing."

"Did you do it? I mean, were you one of the ones who tortured him?"

"I didn't *torture* him, Marc. But, yes, I couldn't help but feel him and test his body. That was one of the reasons I was there, after all. He was very smart, or his trainer was. Someone certainly knew what the attractions to his body were going to be and his sac had been carefully shaven, making the skin seem even smoother and more delicate. The balls themselves actually felt more vulnerable than they would have if his hair had been kept there.

"The next young man had a different attraction. He was blond, smooth skinned with hardly any body hair at all. He was wonderfully tanned. That was highly emphasized where his blond complexion had been covered by a small bathing suit. It left his very nice ass alabaster in contrast to the brown of his legs, stomach and back.

"Just as our attention had been drawn to the other's testicles, this younger and blond man's buttocks drew everyone's attention. There was a strap on each table. Often the buyers want to see how a potential slave will react to a beating. It can be very upsetting to spend a great deal of money for a slave and then discover that he falls apart at the very appearance of a crop or a belt. It's important, some feel, to test out at least some of the reactions.

"The blond was in tears soon enough after a line of the customers had come up and commanded him to lean forward and put his head on the mirrored table so they could each deliver a series of hard blows to the white bottom that was quickly striped with angry red lines."

"So? Who were the other two?"

"They shared the same mirrored table together since they were to be sold as a couple. There was a man and a woman. I wondered about it, very much, but couldn't discover if they were lovers, friends, married or what. They did almost look alike and I had the fantasy that they were a brother and sister. That would have been so perfect that I refused to investigate to see if it was right or wrong. I wanted to make believe that they were, in fact, incestuous and both of them available.

"They received the most attention. That's almost surprising since usually those customers who are homosexually or heterosexually attracted wouldn't have been interested in a mixed couple like that. Or so you would have thought."

"What about you?"

"Me? I've never really limited myself only to men, though you know perfectly well that's my overwhelming desire. But these two, together, were astonishing. They were gorgeous. They both had dark hair, auburn, I think you'd call it. It was cut in nearly identical fashion. It left the man looking vaguely English, the woman slightly masculine. They had very white, pale skin. His body hair wasn't very thick, only a sprinkling on his chest and legs and a thick bunch of it over his cock.

"Their resemblance was accentuated by their kneeling posture. He was larger, but not much. They were perfect on the mirrored table. The contrast and the comparison of the reflections underneath them was amazing.

"They made themselves even more beautiful because they seemed to be in awe of the situation. It was almost as though they hadn't really been able to believe it was going to happen until they discovered themselves naked and on view in front of the guests.

"Their eyes were wide open. They were looking around, almost a little desperately, I thought. While the other two men were resigned to what was going on, these two didn't seem to be. They actually tugged at their chains on a couple occasions, but it was too late to do them any good. There was no escape. They had been given those opportunities before.

"As I said, there was something about the pair that made the two of them the most magnificent of the offerings. They inspired all the guests' imaginations."

"You?"

"Yes, me. It happened this way:

"Madame was entranced by them. She, of course, is much more honestly and equally attracted to both sexes. She had walked — almost glided — up and stood in front of them. They were studying her, looking at her arched eyebrows, that frightening red hair, her proud body. Then, to everyone's astonishment, she simply pulled at the top she was wearing.

"It fell open. She leaned, ever so slightly, towards the two slaves. She didn't have to say a word. Each one of them bent forward and took one of her nipples. They sucked beautifully. At first their eyes were closed, as though they were transported by the joint experience of servicing this beautiful dominatrix.

"I moved behind them. His ass was gorgeous. It was very hard and firm, there were sharp lines in his buttocks and the muscles along his hips. The two halves were separated by the spread of his legs. I looked down on the mirror and could see the hairy growth that protected his anus. Her openings were almost as appealing.

"While they continued their labors with Madame, I reached down and inserted a finger in each of them. One of my hands rested on his ass and probed into that hot, tight hole of his. The other slipped into her vagina. While his had been liberally greased by someone, her lubrication was natural evidence of her own excitement.

"I was amazed by her wetness and the slippery warmth that I could feel. While they gnawed away at Madame, my fingers thrust into them, drawing out these wonderful moans and sighs and groans from the two of them.

"I had to stop finally, only because I was sure that the combination of my and Madame's attention was going to drive the both of them to orgasm. As soon as I did, one of the male slaves of the household was beside me carrying a gold bowl full of soapy warm water with a towel over his arm. The health concerns even move into the slave market, one sees.

"I washed carefully. I was hot, my cock was hard and I was staring at this beautifully near-naked house slave in front of me. While I was standing there, going about the mechanics of washing, he must have felt the intensity of my reactions. Inside his small pouch, he was getting stiff.

"'Only a master can remove it,' he finally said. The tip of his cock was wet from his turn on and had soaked through the fabric, which was in danger of ripping. I thought that was too fine a possibility and chose not to respond to his ill-defined request."

"You just left him there with his hard-on in that silk thing?"

"Yes, I thought it would be more amusing that way."

"You bastard. What happened then?"

"By then, Madame was finished. She had pulled away from the pair of them and was adjusting her top. They were studying her with a real sense of loss on their faces. When they saw me beside her, they had a surge of hope. I think that would be the best word to describe what they were going through.

"I think the two of them suddenly imagined themselves in the hands of a strong woman and a strong man. That would evidently have been the most desirable outcome for them. If they could have, I'm sure they would have begged to be bought by us. But that kind of behavior is strictly forbidden, and I know they would have been told so.

"We simply studied them. We hadn't discussed it, but I know that she and I were pulling off a remarkable event in the eyes of the two slaves. Our severity was certainly having an impact.

"Most often, the male slaves are always erect during one of the sales. If their cocks happen to go down, there's always a way to get them hard again. It wasn't surprising, then, that the male had a hard-on. His cock was very attractive. Not that it was particularly big in a pornographic sense, but it was especially thick, if not noticeably long. It was the kind that made a substantial handle and whose circumference was so great that one had the impression that it was even larger than it was.

"But the male had been more excited than simply that. His cock had begun to leak copiously. There was a long, translucent strand of precome that was seeping from the head in an unbroken line down to the mirrored table top where a good deal of it had gathered in a puddle.

"I reached down and gathered some of it on the tip of each of my forefingers. Then I smeared it on his tits. He closed his eyes — I'll never, ever know if it was shame and distress or ecstasy and delight — the expressions so often appear to be the same in slaves. But I felt as though I had reached in and touched him at some extraordinary level."

"Did you try to buy him?"

"The sale started shortly after that. The four who were being auctioned off had all been examined and so had their papers."

"Papers?"

"Their contracts. I've explained this all to you before. Is it just that you don't believe that people can make these conscious choices? They do. These four people weren't dragged in off some street, they weren't kidnapped.

"They made contracts. Each one had to file a contract with the sponsors. The results were in folders that were attached to the table they were kneeling on. The couple, for instance, agreed to be sold only if they would not be separated. That is an acceptable limitation on them. Each one of them also defines a length of time for his or her slavery. It can be as little as one year. Some I've seen have been as long as ten. But that's allowed only for the experienced and most stable slaves.

"Too often people envision an exciting lifetime of slavery and they forget that there is a whip on the other hand of the master or mistress and that the whip stings. Only contracts that seem to be within the abilities of the slaves are accepted.

"There can be other limitations, but the slaves are clearly told that they risk reducing their value if they demand too many. Still, it can be allowed."

"What? What kinds of agreements can a slave demand?"

"Well, for instance, a slave can announce his profession and have an agreement that he wouldn't be used or displayed to anyone who is a part of it, making sure that he could re-enter his occupation after his contracted period. That can be very important. Or else, some smart and experienced slaves can object beforehand to certain things they feel will make them less valuable in the future: Piercing, for example, isn't considered a permanent mark. Those — permanent marks — aren't allowed under any contract that The Network assigns. But if the slave doesn't specify that piercings are a part of that, they can be performed as a transitory adornment of a slave's body for the duration of the contract."

"You really think that people who buy other people are going to honor these contracts?"

"Of course they are. There is an element of self-monitoring that's very important, for one thing. There's a tremendous screening process as well. Think, Marc, think of the potential scandal and think who some of the people involved are and realize that this must be taken care of internally very carefully and very well.

"I'm not saying that the people who are bought are going to have an easy time of it. They've said that there is a set amount of money that's involved. In exchange for this sum, each one will serve out his or her contract as a total slave to the buyer. They have given up all recourse to any sense of justice other than the master or mistress's pleasure. They certainly are not in control of the situation once they've signed their contracts. I wouldn't deny that at all."

19 &

"If these people have a contract that says that they're going to get a set amount of money, then why is there an auction?"

"Whoever brings them in — the trainer or the recruiter — receives all the money the auction brings above the contract sum."

"Other people are making money on these sales then? If slaves are trained by you, you get the profit, not them?"

"There's a great deal of expense involved in training someone. Look at someone like you and think about the time and energy I'd have to put into you to get you ready for the mirrored tables of the auction room."

"Fuck you!" he answered. I'd hit a sore point. He stood up and went into the house. He came back with a fresh beer, but I could see that the short break hadn't gotten rid of the erection that was fighting against the denim of his jeans.

"So these people — these slaves — they're on the block. What happens now?"

"Now the host comes forward and offers each one for sale. The contract's read out loud. The sums are quite substantial. The money to be made doing this — being a slave — is a great deal more than you make at your mill."

"Don't start," he said. I hadn't really wanted to do any more than prod him a bit and didn't pursue the subject.

"Then, the bids are made. They're done by a code, a simple wave of the hand. The slaves are never allowed to know the monetary sum that's finally agreed upon. It was discovered that they became too arrogant about those things. Better for them to concentrate on their contracted amount. The silent bidding leaves them in a great deal of confusion — it's never explained to them — and we all get to watch the delicious fear on their faces that comes from the terror or the humiliation that their asked-for sum won't be met. That's never happened. There *are* some other fools who say they will go in and be slaves for a year only if they're paid a ridiculously exorbitant amount of money, but they're screened out. It's all done very efficiently and quite fairly. The Network also won't let a slave undervalue himself or herself."

"So, what happened to these four?"

"The first man, the dark one, was sold to a very intriguing Chinese man. I've met him before. He lives in Hong Kong. He's fabulously wealthy from one of those mysterious Chinese banking fortunes. He maintains an incredible harem.

"The male slave actually will have one of the most interesting careers possible. His contract was only for two years. I'm sure he'll beg to be retained for much longer."

"Why? What goes on there? In Hong Kong?"

"The banker lives in a grand mansion. If you or I were to visit, we would see only the luxurious residence of a substantial business-man. But the house is huge. There is a half of it that only the most special guests are ever allowed to see.

"He maintains a household of at least twelve slaves at all times. He prides himself on the make-up; his slaves represent every race possible. There must have been an opening for a Caucasian; that would have been the reason for his visit. He must already have a blond; that would be why he chose this darker-haired man.

"The slaves are kept in utter luxury. They eat the finest food and have incredible facilities. In order to keep in shape, there's a large swimming pool and weight-lifting equipment. There are movies on recorders. There is fine music provided in very formal programs in the evening. If some slaves aren't educated, the others are encouraged to teach them.

"Their only purpose is to be beautiful — and sexual. They are dressed in sheer loose-fitting pants that are gathered beneath the navel and again at the ankles. You can clearly see every part of their bodies.

"They learn the arts of beauty, giving each other pedicures, manicures and so forth, caring for each other's hair. They learn massage and have the most exquisite oils to enhance their odor and to highlight the appearance of their skin.

"They're all encouraged — actually, it's demanded — to have sex with one another as often as possible. The master enjoys watching them at their erotic play. He, of course, also expects that they'll perform any act on him that he ever desires.

"But the man has dedicated his life to beauty. What is most often demanded of his slaves is their exhibition for him. They're tied with silken ropes to the columns of his harem rooms. They wait on him, their nakedness obvious through those sheer clothes. They lay naked across his table while he eats. They are forced into

21 &

remarkably obscene postures for his visual pleasure."

"No whips, no chains?"

"Whips and chains, of course. That's because there's nothing that makes a man look more beautiful than the struggle against real pain and real bondage. Theirs isn't a life without pain. But it's not the harsh life that others live and it's one that's full of pleasure as well. The few times that I've met one of his former slaves, they've always looked back on their years in that Hong Kong mansion as a pleasant dream.

"Any who've left have done so of their own accord. If one outlives his beauty, the master doesn't throw the slave out onto the street. He receives his contract money and then is given a good job in any one of a number of businesses. He inevitably becomes a dramatically loyal and willing employee.

"One of the leading bankers of San Francisco is a man who once spent ten years in Hong Kong. The first five were as a pleasure slave to this millionaire. But, then, the man was allowed to become a business apprentice as well and made the transition that allowed him to head his own company.

"I'm told, though, that he is prone to moods. I'm sure they occur whenever the master from Hong Kong is in the country and the San Franciscan has to remember what he gave up — all that pleasure, the sensuality, the luxury — for the sake of a transitory and not very attractive success in the world of commerce."

"The others? The blond guy?"

"He will have a much more difficult life. Very. He was purchased for a large sum — much larger than I expected — by someone whose true identity is very much hidden. I can only tell you this: He's one of the leading clerics of the country. He demands utter obedience, as the religious usually do. The boy will spend his years under the guise of being a chauffeur or some such thing. That's very common: many of these slaves masquerade in public as paid servants — pilots, nurses, drivers, butlers.

"But the cleric will, I'm sure, keep a devastatingly accurate list of all the slightest mistakes the young man makes every day. Each night he'll find himself under the lash for each one of them. His will be a term of agony. I only hope that that, perhaps, is what he was looking for and, remember, he had to know that this was a possibility."

"Your couple? Did you bid?"

"No. Only because I knew that the money would be much too rich for me. The sum was, in fact, astronomical. A Canadian oil man, a Texas land baron and a woman who's made a fortune selling her own brand of cosmetics got into a bidding war that had heads spinning.

"When it was over, the Canadian had won. Then he put on a spectacle."

"A spectacle? After everything else you've described, what could possibly have gone on that you'd call it that?"

"As each slave is sold, he or she's delivered to the buyer. Most often, it's a very delicate and ritualistic event. The slave is brought down off the mirrored table. The hands are released from the neck chain which is now attached to a leash, and he or she is led, on hands and knees, over to the master.

"The first slave, the dark-haired one, had done it brilliantly. He'd been taken over by the same household slave whose minor agony I'd provided. The Hong Kong banker simply took the leash, bowing gracefully to thank the auctioneer and even the household slave. He'd very delicately pulled on the leash to bring his new purchase in close between his legs. The man had done it very gracefully and was rewarded with a pat on the head. He'd responded by licking the hand of his new master.

"It was quite beautiful.

"The blond went through something similar, but without the affection. That — affection — was something the bishop was never going to give him in any event and he might as well understand that from the beginning.

"But each buyer has the right to establish his or her self to the slave from the very beginning in any fashion. The Canadian evidently wanted the couple to understand their contracted lives very well.

"He had two henchmen with him. When the couple were brought over to the Canadian, he didn't move. But each henchman took one of the leashes. The apartment, which appears to be so stylishly decorated, obviously has its secrets and many of us know them.

"There is a chandelier very close to where the auction had taken place. From it dangle what appear to be ornamental metal ropes. They are, in fact, terrifically strong chains.

"The man and woman were dragged over to them. The men brought out wrist restraints and applied them to the two. In seconds, the male was on his toes, barely able to support his weight, and the woman was hanging from her wrists.

"They brought over a footstool for her. She foolishly thought it was for her relief. But quickly realized that it was just the right height to bring her vagina up to the level of the male's cock. The mystery and the tension had excited him. He was stiffly erect. The henchman slipped a condom over it and roughly shoved the hard cock up the woman's sex.

"Then the two men took off their belts. While the two slaves were fucking, the belts began to fly. The henchmen walked around them in a circle, delivering constant blows to all parts of their mid-sections — their buttocks, their hips, their thighs.

"They were screaming in shock and agony, but they continued their sexual acts. They must have been true masochists. They kept thrusting at one another while the beating went on and on, bringing out bright red welts quickly and sharply.

"Suddenly, the beating stopped. The slaves were released and put back down on the floor. Their tears were ignored while their collars and leashes were reapplied. They weren't even allowed to move on their hands and knees. They had to crawl with their naked bellies on the floor back over to the Canadian who'd bought them.

"When they got there, they were forced to remove his shoes and socks and then to lick, kiss and fondle his feet. Then the two hired men pulled out their cocks, slipped on condoms, and began fucking the slaves.

"One took the male's ass; the other the woman's vagina from the back. This was no easy fucking, let me assure you. This wasn't the sensual delight that the Hong Kong banker was going to be giving the new member of his harem. This was violent, unforgiving, and memorable.

"The Canadian was establishing the ground rules for the next five years."

"Five years," Marc whispered.

"That had been their contract. Five years of service.

"When the two had finished the fucking they yanked the long hair on the two slaves and brought them up to the owner's crotch. His cock was out. It was, quite frankly, enormous. It was one of those uncut *things* that some men have, with long, loose foreskin and very heavy balls underneath it. The two of them, still crying loudly and with tears falling down their faces, were put to work licking and stroking his balls with their mouths and masturbating him with their hands.

"The man came, not caring that his come spilt over his clothing. One of the household slaves was there immediately — his cock hard itself after what he'd witnessed — and went about washing up the Canadian's mess.

"The auctions usually revert to being social events after the actual sales are done. The new slaves are usually left kneeling with their masters and mistresses and are shown off while the food and drink continues, but the Canadian wanted none of that.

"His crying, bruised slaves were exhausted. They could barely move. The henchmen dressed them in nondescript loose clothing and literally carried the two of them out the door and down the elevator — evidently to a waiting car. The Canadian went about only the most essential social niceties, then he too left.

"As you can imagine, Madame and I were beside ourselves after that display. We left shortly. We decided to go to a small party we knew was happening. It had none of the elegance of The Network's affairs, but it provided us with what was — I promise you — *necessary* relief."

Marc was staring at me by the time I'd finished. My term — "necessary relief" — certainly appeared to fit him and his condition. He was so handsome, so wonderfully built, and so obviously receptive to my stories. He could be the answer to my question. I wondered if I needed The Network and its slick operatives and its perfectly trained slaves, or if I only had to think in terms of the raw material with which New England was presenting me.

Eating Conversation

I was only home for a few days. I had explained to Marc that I was going to the Maine coast for a visit. He wanted to get together again soon and I agreed that we'd have dinner when I returned. I wasn't terribly surprised when he asked if his roommate Tim could come along. We set a time and place to meet.

When I walked into the inn, I found the two young men already sitting at the table waiting for me. I greeted them and took my own chair. We made small talk while the waitress was filling our drink orders. I knew that they were wondering where I had been, but I played with them, deciding not to offer the information.

Instead, I asked after their own activities. I learned that both of them had decided to go back to college the coming fall term. They could only afford to attend the local state institution, but they'd correctly determined that any degree would be better than their continued existence as occasional workers. They would have to go to school part-time, but were prepared to make the sacrifice.

"That's wonderful news!" I said. My pleasure was incredible. I couldn't believe what good luck this might be for me. It fit right into my plan. "I'm very proud of you." My congratulations were honestly heartfelt. No matter what happened to my own scheme, this was going to be an excellent move for the young men. They had been having a good life here in the mountains and had been willing to make do with the small earnings they received — Marc in the lumber mill and Tim at seasonal jobs that allowed him to indulge himself with skiing in winter and swimming in the summer. Being gay, they had no pressure to take care of or prepare for a family. They were genial roustabouts, but the flush of their youth would pass and I had often mentioned to them my desire that they have some kind of credential that would allow them some mobility in their future.

Tim seemed to be happy to have my approval. He flushed slightly, looking down into his glass. His full head of hair and his thick moustache were a lighter brown than Marc's. His skin was also ruddier, it was already showing the wear of constant outdoor sports. I knew that the body under his clothes also displayed that conditioning. The times when the two younger men would come to my house and swim in my pond were fond, fond memories.

Marc, though, wasn't able to take praise so easily. "It's not anything big. We'll only go part-time. If it weren't for sharing rent, neither one of us would be able to afford it. We haven't saved anything at all. Big deal, so I'll get a few extra cents on my paycheck out of sitting in a school no one from out-of-state ever heard of."

He finished his drink and waved to the waitress to order another. I nodded when she arrived to indicate that she could bring us a whole round.

"Where have you been?" Marc asked. "To another of your slave auctions?"

Tim flushed again, as though the simple fact of verbalizing those parts of my activities embarrassed him. I stared at Marc for a moment, holding a slight smirk on my face until I was sure he understood that his adolescent behavior hadn't really gotten to me. I had no secrets about my life that these two couldn't know about. In fact, I was pleased that the subject had been brought up so explicitly. I had had every intention of talking to the two of them about it.

"It wasn't a sale at all," I said. I picked up the newly delivered drink. "I had met an old friend when I was at the auction in New York. He invited me to visit his summer home. We had decided it would be best for both of us if I could go this past week."

I studied the two young men. Tim was leaning towards me, his elbows on the table. Marc was sitting back in his chair, one of his arms arrogantly thrown over the back, as though he thought he could signal me that this was not going to be anything so exciting that he had to pay particular attention to it. I was amused by their postures; both of them were obviously more intensely interested than they were ready to admit.

I sipped my drink, savoring the story I was going to be telling them, not only for the reactions that I was sure they'd have, but also because the memory was so perfect.

"The visit was really very wonderful. My host was able to provide an extraordinary hospitality.

"His summer estate is on an island. I drove to the isolated area where he had told me I would be met. It was a deserted pier well off the main roads. I soon learned the reason for the privacy.

"At the appointed time, a long boat appeared. I had expected a powerlaunch, perhaps even a sailboat. But, instead, a rowboat came to the pier. It was a large one, the size of a lifeboat on a sea-going vessel, I would expect. It was powered by four men — obviously slaves he'd bought at auction, or so I had assumed.

"All four were handsome. They were wearing only the type of slim racing brief that I see the two of you wearing on the beach in summer."

Marc shifted on his seat in reaction to the idea that anything he did habitually could be similar to the behavior of a slave. Tim, I noticed, didn't appear to be bothered at all, simply intrigued.

"There was a pair on each of two wooden seats, each with one large oar in his hands. They used the implements very profession-ally. In the prow of the boat was a man much larger than the rest of them. He had the bulk of a professional weightlifter. The rest were obviously following his commands. But his size and the reactions of the four rowers weren't the only proof of his having a different status than they.

"His appearance and clothes were different. His hair was longer, much longer; theirs was very close-cropped. There was a wide leather sweat-band around his head to hold back the thick locks. He was the only one who had a very full beard. Rather than a bathing suit, he had on a pair of white cotton slacks and a pull-over shirt.

"The boat was expertly brought up to the dock. The largest one greeted me very formally and I could hear that his voice was deep and masculine. He bowed slightly when he greeted me. This was also a slave, I realized, but one with a different purpose in the household than the four scantily clad males who ran on his orders to collect my luggage from my car.

"I was seated at the prow of the boat for the return trip. I was amused by the idea of what the vacationers who lived closely would think if they understood what went on in this private enclave.

"My comfortable seat allowed me to study the hard muscles in the slaves' backs as they struggled to follow the orders to 'Stroke!' the larger one yelled out to them. Their purpose was only to provide the propulsion for the craft; he controlled its direction with a rudder that he held firmly in his hands.

"The four men worked hard to fight against the sea. It took quite a while to get to the private island — I would say at least an hour. During that time they labored constantly. I felt Olympian sitting there and watching their tight, hard bodies struggling so hard to carry me to my destination."

The waitress returned to get our dinner orders. I broke off my story and read my choices from the menu, being careful not to allow a hint of discomfort with the interruption. I wanted the two young men who were with me to realize just how matter-of-factly I could relate this tale to them.

Marc had no such ease about them. He was overtly nervous. He seemed to have forgotten the menu was already in front of him and then answered the woman's questions about dressings and choice of potato with quick, almost sharp responses. Tim actually seemed to be calm. He was staring at me while Marc dealt with the waitress and then simply stated that he'd have the same dishes as I.

When she left, I continued:

"We got to the island and the five men and I walked onto the pier there. The muscled man came up to me and said that he would have to wash the others and change himself. I, of course, didn't really understand what he meant, but nodded my agreement to his real point: That I would have to wait just a moment before we went to the house.

"While I stood there, the four other men quickly got underneath a shower that was hooked up to the outside of the very small building that stood at the foot of the wharf. There was a shower outside it, in the open. The pipes must have been hooked up to a fresh water well. The water was certainly not heated. I could tell that by the way the four of them shivered under the spray. But they did wash thoroughly. It was almost a shame. I had been luxuriating in the odors of the sweat that I could smell coming from their labor even over the sea-spray.

"I was also able to watch the transformation of the overseer. He had quickly taken off his full set of clothing and stood naked while he carefully put it away in a cabinet just inside the door of the closet-sized building.

"When he was nude, I could see why he wore clothing when he was off the island, even when he just went to the private pier to pick up guests. Both his nipples were pierced. There were also thick gold rings running through the head of his cock, at its base where it met his testicles and then, again, in his perineum — that area between his scrotal sac and his anus."

The idea of the piercings broke through Marc's facade of nonchalance. He squirmed in his seat. "Why? Why would he have done that?"

"I didn't know that he had been the one to decide it. But, in any event, there are many reasons for the piercings. Many people find them highly erotic — on themselves, or on others. They can be convenient on a slave, as you'll soon see."

"Convenient?" Tim spoke now. He was wide-eyed with fascination.

At that moment, our food arrived. When the waitress had left, I finally answered the question. "Let me go on with my story and you'll understand their potential utility.

"What's even more interesting about him was the outfit he proceeded to put on. First, there were wide leather strips similar to his head band which went around his biceps, obviously they were used to emphasize his build. Then he put on a loin cloth. It was a band of the same leather, no more than four inches wide, gathered at his waist by a piece of rawhide. The flaps hung down at least a foot and a half in the front and in the back. Finally, he put on sandals with straps which wound up his calves.

"The whole impression was something close to barbaric, certainly primeval. The other four males were drying off by now, their shower had finished. I could see the way they studied the brute that the costume had the additional effect of making him seem quite frightening to them.

"He snapped his fingers and they instantly responded by picking up my bags and starting up the hill. Many owners like to have pampered slaves. These men were not. I could tell by the quick and effortless way they walked up the hill over the rocky path in their barefeet. They were used to hard labor, I had also seen that in the way they had handled the oars in the boat.

"I followed them. In a short while we came to the house. It was large and, if unexceptional, it had been meticulously maintained. It was a white clapboard affair. Around it, on the small plateau where the house sat, were handsome gardens. The lawn was a beautiful and even green. It had to be very difficult to keep it up on the island with the constant salt air."

"Amazing what you can do with slave labor," Marc said snidely.

"Isn't it?" I answered, smiling while I chewed on a morsel of veal.

I went on. "My host was waiting on his porch to greet me. I, of course, know who he is in the world. He holds one of the world's most prestigious chairs in philosophy at a major university. But his real fame, for me, comes from the solid and manly way he has maintained a household of males through the years.

"The academic calendar helps, obviously. He has the summer months for intense dedication to his slaves as well as a full month around the holidays when he transports them all to another island retreat, in the West Indies. The rest of the year he keeps them in various capacities in his home. He uses a vast array of false premises to cover their actual purposes.

"I mentioned that to the professor when we were sitting on the porch enjoying a cup of tea. Why, I wondered, hadn't he ever had any of them pass as his students?"

Again, the parallel to their own lives made both Marc and Tim move in their seats. They shot each other glances that almost seemed to carry abject fear in them. But, I thought, that was probably wishful thinking on my part.

"My question amused the professor and deeply upset the man who was waiting on us. I could see that in the way he became suddenly flustered and his body stiffened. I had watched this young man at the oars earlier. He was a fine specimen, tall with broad shoulders and noticeably firm thighs. His reddish hair had obviously been bleached nearly blond in the summer sun on his chest and legs as well as his head.

"The professor quickly explained that this young man was in fact one of his students. 'Not one, by the way, that was purchased at auction, rather one who understood the finest points of pedagogy rather independently.'"

"Not purchased?" Marc said. "You mean, he was volunteering to do all this?"

"Yes, so the professor explained. They had been introduced when the young man had been an undergraduate. He had been a remarkable student and had risen to the top of his class with hard work and careful listening to his teachers. Still he had, so he told the professor, a hard time dealing with the structure of the university. That had surprised the educator. Students who do well seldom understand the flaws of institutions that seem to reward them with good grades.

"But the school was too liberal, too lacking in structure and limits. The student could discipline himself to study and he had learned how to study — something you'll find important yourselves when you go back to school. But the whole of it wasn't satisfying to him.

"There were then a number of other meetings. In some of them, it became obvious that the student was gay. Then, through a mutual friend, the professor and his soon-to-be charge realized that they had a common interest in the more advanced areas of sexuality.

"Over a period of time, they came to an understanding. What the student wanted, really, was an opportunity to serve and to learn that part of himself as well. During the academic year he lived alone. Neither was willing to take the chance of merging their personal and professional lives, and since the young man went on to become a graduate student in the professor's department, they agreed that he would have to keep to that role during those months.

"But, when the professor transported his household to one of his island retreats, the student came along and transported himself into the new world of sexual service."

"Slavery," Marc said in a tone that conveyed his insistence on using the harsher word.

"Slavery," I agreed, finishing off my meal and refusing to be caught in his word games.

"A graduate student?" Tim seemed intrigued with that part of the story more than any other. "I thought they'd all just be . . . bums, people who couldn't make it any other way."

"Oh, no, don't think that. In fact, most masters would insist on an exceptionally intelligent slave. Only one who can understand the extreme complexities of that life can provide the master with the subtleties and the levels of understanding and experience that are needed.

"Another time — perhaps — I'll tell you about the types of men who end up on The Network's auction block. But, for now, let me tell you the rest of this story.

"It proved to be a perfect time for me to have humiliated the young man with my questions. The professor explained that he was being punished that night. It was not going to be a sexual event. There wouldn't be any of the enjoyable aspects of it to help him make his way through the penalty. The professor apologized, actually, saying that it was too bad he couldn't offer me the opportunity to explore the graduate student's many pleasures. But this was a serious event, a response to a number of incidents and, worse, to the young man's attitude."

"What does that mean?" Tim asked.

"The young man had finished his class work for his doctorate. He has only to write his thesis to receive his degree. That will probably take him at least another two years since he's chosen a particularly difficult area to investigate. He was proud of his achievements — too proud. He evidently had arrived at the island and had rebelled at the role which was his once the party reached the retreat. The professor wasn't going to allow that.

"He told me that the graduate student seemed to go through this every summer, though this was the most serious time so far. The young man forgot his place; he'd argue with the muscled one who, I learned, the professor called his 'major domo.' He'd also try to lord it over the other three men, thinking they were somehow inferior because they had been purchased on the block."

"Well, isn't he right? He at least had chosen to be with this old guy," Marc insisted.

"No. A slave may never forget that there is only one choice:

33

To be a slave. When that's made, then all of them are the same, of equal status, except for any finer distinctions that the master might allow for one reason or another.

"Slaves are always forgetting themselves in that way. It's one reason that we've all learned never to let them understand how much money passes hands in their sales. They always try to establish a hierarchy by their value. Any man who has signed any contract has to understand that he is simply a slave and that only his master may determine whether he has any power over the others.

"The professor and I understood this. I also understood that the professor must have been facing a dilemma. If this rebellion was truly an annual event, it could be that the young man was only trying to provoke him into giving out the punishment. That's another common slave game that masters must watch out for."

"For someone to *provoke* punishment?!" Marc was incredulous.

"Of course. Some are, after all, masochists for the most part and enjoy their punishments to some extent. There's also the fact that slaves enjoy the attention."

"Attention?" Marc asked. He was giving up his charade of indifference and had leaned his elbows on the table after our plates had been cleared.

"You must understand that slaves lust for attention and they receive it. Think, *think* of every story I've told you and realize just how much the slave is the centerpiece of each one. He has the undivided consideration of all the others who are with him. He is on the table and being examined. In sex, his body is the one that is being stimulated the most. Yes, of course, they are the ones in the spotlight.

"And it's done in a manner far more overt than ever happens in the rest of society, certainly in terms of how society relates to males."

"Pierced tits are a hell of a price to pay for some attention," Marc said, trying to regain his stance of disinterest.

"Don't make me go too far. That comes later in the story.

"After we'd had our tea, I went to my room and showered and changed clothes for dinner. The professor is a gentleman of the old school and prefers his male guests to dress formally. My bags had been unpacked by some of the slaves and my tuxedo had already been pressed for me. It was waiting on a standing valet in the room.

"I went down at the requested hour and had a fine meal with the old man. It was served by all four of the other men at one time or another. They clearly had their tasks divided equally."

"Naked?" Tim asked. "Were they naked?"

"No, no. They wore very, very slight coverings. They were, I suppose, the same g-strings that strippers wear, though I hate equating them with the vulgarity of the public stage. They're very utilitarian in many ways. They really serve the purpose of making the slave feel even more naked than he would if he were nude. The small, gripping piece of fabric around his genitals and the string that constantly rubs against his anus are constant reminders of his sexual purpose. Too, they make sure that a guest won't be bothered with the unwanted contact with the slave's cock.

"Though, of course, a guest could easily remove the cup if he wanted to."

"Did you?" Tim asked again.

"Not at dinner," I smiled when I answered him.

"There was, though, a tension. The man the professor called the major domo was still in his leather trappings. He stood guard over the dining room and when I looked up I could see that he was studying the graduate student. I soon learned why: The professor explained that the major domo would be administering the punishment.

"That, of course, was to underline the purpose. If the professor had been wielding the whip, it might have been possible for the penitent to imagine the actions as something of personal value between himself and his master. That's another of the games the slaves use to undermine their masters' attempts to chastise them."

"You make it seem so difficult to be a master, what with all this work you have to do to outguess your subjects." Marc was trying to spar with me again.

I smiled just as easily as I had before: "Trust me, it is intellectually exhausting."

I let the two of them sit with that answer for a moment before I continued. "The punishment was to take place immediately after we had our coffee. The professor led me to the front lawn. There were chairs waiting there for us. Another of the slaves brought us brandy — I should say, a fine cognac. The professor would never serve mere brandy.

"There had been other preparations made as well. For one thing, there was a bonfire all set up, only waiting to be lighted. More ominous, a frame of heavy wood had been constructed. The major domo had been busy while the professor and I had chatted and I had been dressing.

"He was waiting for us outdoors. As soon as we arrived, he started the kindling underneath the wood. Then the professor made some signal. The five slaves came out of the house. The three who were only going to witness this event — or so they thought — walked to one side of the area and sat down on the grass. The major domo roughly grabbed the upper arm of the offender and dragged him over to where the two of us sat. He threw him forward, so harshly that the graduate student lost his footing and sprawled unceremoniously at our feet.

" 'You may leave, Daniel,' the professor said. This was the first time I had heard the slave's name.

"At first he thought he was being given an opportunity to simply escape his punishment. But he quickly understood that the professor meant that he could leave everything. He was free to depart the island and this entire life. When that realization hit, sheer panic swept over him. Daniel crawled forward on his belly and grabbed the older man's foot and began kissing it. He moaned, 'No, please, not that, no, let me stay with you . . . ,'

" 'Then accept my authority, both tonight with this punishment and in the future in every way I demand it.'

" 'Yes, please, of course . . . ,'

"The professor motioned to the major domo. He came and grabbed hold of Daniel again, then dragged him to the wooden frame. I looked over at the other three and knew that they dreaded the thing. There was such a strong reaction evident on their faces that I was sure they had all had their experiences with it in the past.

"The major domo was quick and efficient as he tied Daniel's wrists and ankles to the extremities of the posts. He took up a thick piece of leather which had holes drilled through it at regular intervals. The professor obviously meant this to be an intense lesson.

Those holes meant that each blow would leave a pattern of blisters wherever the bludgeon hit.

"The fire was roaring by now. It sent up utterly demonic lights around the whole circle of us. The major domo ripped the small covering off Daniel. When he did, even though our angle wasn't awfully good, I could see that the slave was erect, his cock speared out of his belly into the air. It was proof that the professor had been right to insist that this punishment be as harsh as possible. Daniel would, indeed, have turned it into a personal sexual event if he had been given any chance at all.

"The major domo went to work without any of the easy preliminaries that one might use with a slave during a pleasurable scene. The piece of leather leapt through the air, the holes made whooshing sounds for those split seconds before it thudded into Daniel's skin.

"He howled from the first blow. I could only imagine the agony involved. The major domo kept up the blows, carefully altering the target so he could inflict the major amount of pain without really damaging Daniel, or allowing the young graduate student to anticipate where the next attack would strike.

"I thought it had ended, realizing that it was over rather quickly since there had been no finesse involved in the punishment. Daniel's buttocks were a mass of red, there were deeply scarlet circles where the holes in the paddle had hit, the rest of his ass had less violent evidence of the torture. But, I was wrong. The major domo wasn't finished. Now he took out a cat-o'-nine-tails. He let the implement cut through the air before he turned it on the still crying slave.

"The cat was used on Daniel's back. It cut carefully designed stripes on those same broad shoulders that I had seen in the boat. It was, I knew, not as brutally painful as the other beating had been, but it was much more mentally devastating. It always is. Men are more able to suffer pain on their buttocks. Physically, there's more protection; psychologically, it's easier to take. But a whipping on the shoulders is more demeaning, more humiliating.

"The cat was also used elsewhere, and this time for pain. When he was satisfied that Daniel's back had suffered enough, the major domo took the long lashes and attacked the back of the slave's legs. That's one of the most vulnerable parts of the human body. Only the truly knowledgeable master understands just what agony a slave receives from punishments that are inflicted there."

"All the secrets of the trade," Marc muttered.

I continued to play with him: "There are more. The soles of the feet, for instance, are even more tender, obviously the stomach is as well, though one must use optimal care not to do real damage there. I happen to prefer the insides of the thighs. There's always the added danger that the lash might wander a bit too high and hit the slave's balls. That fear in the slave, combined with the exquisite pain that's possible in that part of his anatomy, produces the maximal result in my opinion.

"In any event, the major domo was finally finished with his duties. He looked to the professor who nodded his permission to end the punishment.

"Daniel was released from the frame. The sweat that had collected on his body reflected the flames of the bonfire beautifully and made it actually increase the visual impression of the deep red evidence of his whipping. He fell to the ground, utterly exhausted. The major domo prodded him with his foot, though, and wouldn't let him rest.

"Daniel was forced to crawl over to the professor. As soon as he arrived at his master's chair, he once again began to kiss his feet in a display of deep homage. The professor didn't even acknowledge the slave's obeisance. He reached into his coat pocket and brought out a handful of wrapped condoms. He threw them over Daniel's head onto the lawn.

"'Go and fetch one. Take it to Joseph,' the old man commanded. Daniel seemed to panic all over again. He stared up at his master as though silently begging him to avoid this one punishment. But there was no forgiveness in the professor's face and there was the major domo with the cat still in his hand standing close by.

"Daniel turned and crawled to the middle of the lawn where he found one of the condoms. He picked it up in his mouth and, still crawling, carried it that way to one of the other slaves.

"This, obviously, was Joseph. Daniel laid the packet down at the other slave's crossed feet. 'Use it any way that you desire,' the professor said. Joseph smiled broadly and grinned at the other two. He stood up and pulled aside his covering. He had a magnificent cock, one of those that is circumcised, but still shaped perfectly. The knob was in proportion to the already hardening shaft. His testicles were very handsome, two large eggs wrapped beautifully in dark hair.

"He was as well built as Daniel, and about the same age, twenty-five. Daniel followed his orders and removed the latex condom from its wrappings. He carefully unrolled it on Joseph's now stiff cock. Then, still following orders, Daniel began to suck on the tightly wrapped organ.

"The other slaves, of course, loved this. They crowded around the kneeling figure and began to yell at him, claiming he wasn't doing the job adequately, saying that he never would learn, would he? They took hold of his head and forced it further down on Joseph's cock until Daniel began to seriously gag on the large erection. Only then would they allow him to move backwards for air and they sternly admonished him not let the head of Joseph's cock free."

"Great friends," Marc said with a sneer.

Tim didn't say anything, but I thought I saw a flicker of pain run over his face. Then I remembered Marc's stories about his friend. There had been experiences in Tim's past. I would have to find out more about them. They had seemed — from the little Marc had told me — to be simple enough. But his reactions tonight appeared to be so complex.

"Oh, everyone in this world understands that there is nothing more vicious than another slave," I continued. Tim actually grimaced when he heard me make that observation. "That was assuredly one reason that the professor had designated the large one his major domo. A master's punishment might be feared — and usually with good cause — but even it would pale beside the image of one slave having power over another, especially if the one being punished had put on airs and claimed to be better than the others, which is precisely what Daniel had done.

"Finally, Joseph couldn't hold back his orgasm and it grabbed hold of his entire body, sending spasms through his muscles and a flood of come into the latex.

"The professor ordered Daniel to return to the middle of the circle and retrieve still another condom in his mouth. The fire was still roaring and now it caught the streams of tears that were flooding down the graduate student's cheeks. But, of course, he complied.

"This time Daniel took the packet to a slave they called Jose. He was clearly Hispanic with curly black hair and a silky smooth complexion. He was laughing with pleasure as he watched Daniel bring the present to him. He was intent on inflicting as much humiliation on Daniel as possible. He forced him to kneel with his back to him, then to put his forehead on the grass. Daniel followed his next order and reached behind himself and spread the substantial halves of his buttocks so that Jose was given a completely open target for a fucking which proved to be hard and harsh.

"The last slave was named Benjamin. He was a strikingly handsome blond man, the rare type who has a great deal of yellow body hair. He looked slightly older than the rest, I would say he might have been thirty. He wanted to humiliate Daniel as well. But he didn't choose to do it in the brutal fashion of the others. Instead, he stood over the kneeling Daniel and, not even using the offered condom — its protection wasn't going to be necessary — he had his fellow slave reach up with his tongue and use it to lick at his balls. He also ordered Daniel to lift his arms up and manipulated his tits. While he was receiving all this attention, the slave masturbated a very lovely cock, the largest in the group from what I could see.

"He sent his orgasm's fluid showering in thick waves onto Daniel's back. When he'd regained himself, he laughed and then rubbed his deposit into the graduate student's skin. The others joined him in thinking this was a fine joke. They took their condoms and emptied them onto Daniel.

"Then it was the major domo's turn.

"Daniel was even more exhausted by now, though his erection was also back again. He crawled to the muscular behemoth and dropped the packet on the ground in front of him. The major domo handed it back to Daniel. He waited patiently, with his enormous arms crossed over his chest, while the kneeling figure once again was forced to put on another man's condom.

"Then the giant slave had Daniel sprawl out on his back with his arms and legs extended. He took a position over the vulnerable, smaller slave similar to one that you'd use for sixty-nine. But he, of course, had no intention of taking Daniel's cock in his mouth. Nor was he going to be satisfied with a simple sucking by Daniel either.

"Instead, he began movements that can only be described as fucking Daniel's mouth. He used his ferocious hips to pile drive his cock down Daniel's throat. Daniel's posture had obviously been designed to give the major domo the best angle for the deepest penetration.

"Taking the man's cock must have been excruciating. It was clear, for one thing, that Benjamin did not have the largest one of the group. The size of the major domo's erection was proportionate to the rest of his muscles. But Daniel had no choice in the matter in any event. His body was trapped under the big man's bulk and he couldn't move at all. He had to take the constant thrusts that the other one forced down him.

"Mercifully, the major domo didn't take too long to come. I'm not at all sure how long Daniel could have taken the attack. When it was over and the major domo stood up over him and took off his condom, Daniel was left choking on the ground; his hands had flown to his throat as though he could protect it from the assault that was now already over with.

"He had certainly been more brutally used than he had been by any of the others."

The waitress came back and broke the spell that I seemed to be weaving in Marc and Tim's minds. She offered us coffee and after-dinner drinks. I declined and instead offered to serve both back at my own house where we could avoid these interruptions.

Marc eyed me with a look of distrust, but Tim was clearly interested in anything that would let the tales continue.

Sven

We drove the short distance to my house in separate cars. I was pleased — even excited — by the reaction my stories were receiving from my two young friends. I cautioned myself to calm down and not rush any of the plans I had formulated on that island retreat with the professor. I could lose too much if I were to become over-anxious.

They arrived shortly after me. I had put on the coffee and had lighted the fire that was already prepared in the hearth. They took chairs in the living room and stared at the flames. I wondered if they were being reminded about the bonfire on the island. I was.

"So, Daniel got his punishment." Marc finally broke the silence after I had brought in the coffee pot and cups and had then delivered a selection of liqueurs and glasses. I didn't respond until all three of us had gotten our beverages.

"Yes, he did. It was quite effective. At the end of the evening he was kneeling at the professor's feet with his head on the older man's lap. His body was covered with various bruises and his face was swollen from his tears. Eventually the major domo took him away and it was obviously time for bed."

"After all this, you went to bed alone?" Tim asked.

"Of course not. The vision of Daniel kneeling at the feet of the blond man and licking his balls while playing with his nipples had seemed very enticing to me. I decided Benjamin should show me just how pleasurable an act it could be. I had been assured that any of the slaves were mine for the asking. They had obviously been told the same thing and he didn't hesitate when I indicated that I wanted him showered and ready in my room at once.

"It was a pleasant night. He was extremely grateful that I didn't want anything more exotic and he performed the simple acts I requested with a certain gusto. I had him spend the night with me so he could repeat them in the morning and then go fetch my coffee so I could enjoy it in bed."

"He was yours for the rest of the week?" Tim asked.

"No, no. I had my pick of them all. The four young men — the oarsmen — were there in those skimpy costumes whenever I wanted for whatever I wanted and I did use them occasionally. But they were not the most intriguing option I had. I was much more interested in the major domo.

"Over breakfast the next morning, the professor assured me that his offer of my pick of his slaves included the overseer. He was even a little taken aback that I had even asked, but I had thought it prudent since the man obviously had a special status in the household.

"I said I wanted to watch him work out. I correctly assumed he had to have a regular regime in order to have developed that awesome physique. It turned out that the major domo was scheduled to be in his gymnasium at that very moment. Rather than interfere with my meal, the professor sent Joseph running to tell him to stop whatever he had done and wait for me to arrive.

"I learned a bit about him from the professor. The major domo's name was Sven. His dark hair had misled me, I hadn't realized that he was Scandinavian. He had come to the professor via The Network at a very young age — so young it embarrassed the older man to admit that he had bought Sven the day he had turned eighteen. He had been waiting impatiently for his age of majority in order to mount The Network's stages and the organizers, admiring his persistence and drive, had even accommodated him by scheduling a sale on his birthday.

"Sven had a number of stipulations on his contract. They were hardly onerous to a master; in fact, they were quite appealing. One was that he be allowed to pursue his desire to be a competitive body-builder. Another, that he receive a college education; that's how I learned that Daniel wasn't the only one who fit into the role of student to the professor's mentor.

"Sven had gladly gone with the professor and had thrown

himself into both his priorities. He had displayed a tremendous loyalty to the older man. When the degree had been earned and the physique title he had worked for had been won, Sven had come to his master and asked for a remarkable contract: a contract for the rest of his life.

"That was arranged and the sale money was put into a special account so that Sven would be quite a rich man when the professor passed on. As a symbol of that step in their relationship, Sven had begged the professor for the piercings that he wore now. Since he was no longer going to compete professionally, he could afford to have his body adorned in that way as a gift to his master. He got them and he got the position of major domo in the professor's household.

"I was surprised that Sven was only twenty-six. I would have thought him older. But it was a question of his size and his and the professor's desire that he have the image of a barbaric warrior with the clothing and the hair to go with it.

"I had that information when I went to the training room. Sven and I were left alone and I was able to see something very handsome and appealing waiting for me. There was Sven, standing awkwardly and wearing only an athletic supporter. He was no longer the major domo lording it over the others. He was now just another slave waiting for a master and wondering and worrying just what it was that the master would want from him.

"He bowed when I entered and kept his eyes lowered to the floor. I told him I would watch his workout. I asked if his routine was written down. He said it was and went and got a sheet of paper. I saw that it was written in the professor's hand and knew that it must have been something the two of them had devised together.

"There was a whole set of different exercises and varying athletic events that Sven would do depending on the day of the week. I was pleased that I had chosen this evidently 'easy' day. While it would have been pleasurable to witness his struggle with the enormous free-weights that I saw neatly stacked in the corners, today's gymnastic rituals were more promising.

"He began doing a few stretching exercises. They were remarkably obscene, of course, with deep bends at the waist that exposed his anus.

"He did a few more aerobic actions to get himself ready and then started on his sit-ups. I sat and watched the huge bulk of his flesh as it began to puff up in response.

"You must understand: The other four slaves had great bodies. They obviously worked hard and they, too, probably worked out in this room. But their builds were those that we see in magazines: Sleek, hard and lined. But Sven was of a different order. He looked the part of the barbarian as a Hollywood director would cast him. His body was enormous and the muscles weren't the symmetrical visual delights of the others; each piece of his flesh was a component of a powerful machine.

"I walked over to him. I stood next to him and knelt down, just to be closer and to be able to smell the masculine odor of the sweat that was beginning to come out of his pores. His eyes darted to see where I was and what I was doing, but he continued his motions.

"I put out a hand and felt the surface of his skin as he worked. There was a slight stubble on his chest. Obviously he kept his body shaved. He was successful as he tried to keep his concentration while I touched him. He accepted the explorations I made on his body as my due while he continued working.

"He shifted after a time and began to do push-ups. I stopped him. He froze and looked at me, wondering what I could possibly want. I remembered that the professor was a great game fisherman. I told him to fetch the old man's box for me. He was puzzled, but ran to get what I had asked for.

"I rummaged through it. I found a handful of small lead weights. They're used to help sink a line. They have tiny hooks attached to them. I smiled and told Sven that I doubted he really needed the supporter to do such simple exercises. He didn't hesitate to take off the elastic garment.

"All of his piercings were exposed now. I walked over to him and he sucked in his breath as he watched me attach two of the small weights to each of his nipple rings. Then I put two on each of his genital rings as well. They were heavy enough to tug at this flesh, though they couldn't tear it. When I was satisfied with my little body decorations I told him to resume his push-ups.

"It became a perfect scene. Each time Sven would lift his huge body up off the floor, the weights would drag at his cock, his balls and his nipples. He was in a sensual agony with the constant cycle of stress and relaxation that my devices caused and soon his cock was fully erect.

"When he moved to begin a series of pull-ups on a bar there in the room, I removed the weights. At first he was happy, but then he saw what I had really intended for him. I took a piece of fishing line from the professor's box and tied it around his cock and balls. I measured his height exactly and then attached the other end to a weight that I left on the floor. Now, every time that Sven chinned himself, he would have to lift up the weight with his genitals. Again, there wasn't enough to cause any damage, I was careful about that. But the pain wasn't the slight and erotic sensation that he'd gotten from the tiny lead pieces on his rings. It was much more intense and made it much more difficult for him to accomplish his feats.

"In fact, he nearly rebelled at one point. I shouldn't say that; rebellion isn't what he would do. Rather, he nearly got to the point where the essentially self-inflicted pain was so horrible that he could barely bring himself to perform the act that would bring it on. But, he did, in fact, accomplish the required number of repetitions.

"When he was done with the pull-ups I told him I wanted a glass of wine. He said that, of course, he would get it for me. But then he realized that I hadn't removed the weight that was still tied to his cock and balls. I had no intention of doing so. I stared at him until he realized that I was purposely leaving him with his metal burden. He knew enough to not even ask if it would be permissible to lift it up off the floor; I obviously meant for him to drag it.

"He walked from the weight room into the kitchen — a good distance — and returned presently with my drink. I sipped it while he stood there. I raised my leg and used my foot to stretch the wire taut. He squeezed his eyes shut with the sudden pain and then let the pressure I was applying direct him downward onto his knees in front of me."

"He must have hated you," Marc said. He had finished his drink and took a bottle to pour himself another.

"Hated me? Hardly. I think that was the moment when he fell in love with me."

"How could he?" Tim asked. His eyes were wide open and he seemed almost frightened to know.

I left the question unanswered and went back to my story about Sven: "I let him up after a bit and finally removed the bondage around his cock and balls. I had thought of an interesting next step. I asked him if the list of that day's routine was all that he could do. He assured me it was simply a minimal requirement that the professor expected of him. That was what I had supposed.

"I told him I would like to see him work with some of the weights. He agreed readily, though he said it would be necessary for him to use his supporter again and, depending on what I expected of him, one of those thick leather belts that are used to protect a weightlifter's back. I told him to get himself ready while I went looking for something special.

"Jose was in the kitchen. He told me where I could find the sanitized dildos that the professor kept for his own and other people's amusement with the slaves. I was able to enjoy a few seconds of terror on his face. He thought I meant to use them on him. But I went to the closet and retrieved one that suited my purposes perfectly. It wasn't terribly thick, but it was quite long.

"I had Jose find me a hammer and nails. I took it all back to the training room. I hammered the base of the dildo onto a wooden stool I had seen there. It was only about a foot tall and was primarily for decorative appearances. I had also gotten a jar of lubricant and covered the dildo's rubber skin with grease. Sven realized at once what was happening. I placed my little piece of manufacture in the center of the weight area and resumed my seat. I poured myself another glass of wine and didn't have to say a word to him. He understood what I expected.

"He had put a number of the biggest weights on the bar. I think he was probably trying to impress me with his strength though I'm sure he regretted his little act of bravado at that moment. But he was resigned. He proceeded to do what they call squats. The weight-lifter holds a huge amount of weight behind his back and then bend his knees to lower his body as far as he can and then to once again lift up himself and the weights.

"But, of course, Sven had an added sensation. Every time he lowered himself, he impaled his ass on the waiting dildo. He had to fuck himself over and over again to do the exercises. It left him breathless and quite excited. He was stiff and there were wet spots on his supporter by the time he was finished.

"I was quite pleased with his performance. I told him that we could stop now. He should go and shower. He came back quickly; he hadn't even taken much time to towel off and his hair was still wet. He stood in front of me and waited for my next command. He was obviously interested in what it might be since his cock was hard. It was the kind that I like. It wasn't circumcised. I've said it was large, though bulk isn't always that important in a cock. I prefer that they look appealing more than anything else. I like to have a substantial knob on the head. I'm not one who desires extra layers of foreskin. On the contrary, I like it to be nicely molded to the knob, just a comfortable sheath. I like to see the veins on the shaft stand out, and not to have so much hair on it that you lose much of the image of a strong penis, especially when it's erect. Sven's cock was really exceptional, to my taste. It had all the right qualities.

"I got up and ran my hand over his body. I told him that I could see he needed it taken care of. If I could feel that stubble, it must be time for it to be shaved again. He nodded and went to get the razor and cream. He stood with his hands behind his neck and his legs spread while I applied the lotion to any part of his body where there might have been hair at one time or another."

"Didn't he have any?" Marc asked.

"Yes, actually, there had been a triangle left to crown the top of his cock and balls. But he had no good answer when I asked him if that was necessary, so I shaved that as well. When I was done he had only the thick beard and the long hair on the top of his head."

"You were trying to emasculate him, weren't you? I've read that, that shaving a man is like cutting off his cock." Marc made his declaration seriously. I waved his complaints away.

"How could people ever think such things? When I was standing there and enjoying the feel of his big cock, how do you think I was trying to cut it off, even symbolically? That's foolishness. I think the better way to understand the act is to conceive of my grooming a very valuable and very handsome thoroughbred. I was treating Sven just that way.

"He and I both knew that his body was remarkable. He had spent half his life making it that way. Of course he wanted it to be cared for and appreciated. I was helping do what he wanted. I was removing the hair that would hide the superb muscles he'd developed and those that nature had given him as well.

"There is a sense of danger that any slave must feel when he's being shaved. I know that. Sven was watching the long sharp straight-edge razor carefully, especially when it approached his nipples and his cock and balls. There is no denying the master's power at a moment like that. But I was talking to him the whole time, giving him deserved credit for the cords of muscle in his thighs and arms and buttocks. He was receiving a continuing line of praise from me.

"It firmly established many things between us. I moved on to make sure that there were even more levels of understanding. I was attracted to Sven; I also thought I knew things that he wanted, even needed."

"What an ego you have!" Marc said with a hint of challenge in his voice. He was agitated enough to pour himself yet another drink.

"Ego? I have certain knowledge that's been acquired, that's all."

"How?" Tim asked that question quickly. I ignored it and went on with my story.

"I told Sven that he could get me my lunch and that he should bring his own portion with him and join me on the lawn. He was delighted and started to put on his leather clothing. That, I informed him, wasn't what I desired. Didn't he have one of the small g-strings that the others wore? He did, though he blushed when he admitted it. I ordered him to wear it while he served my meal.

"The sun was bright and warm. There was a nice breeze off the ocean, but it wasn't chilly the way it can be off the Maine coast. I was in a chaise longue and enjoying the sun when Sven came back out with a tray.

"I'd changed and was only wearing a pair of swimming trunks. No matter how beautiful his own body was, there was no doubt that Sven looked at me with undisguised lust. I was very taken aback by it, actually. I enjoyed it, of course, but I hadn't expected it.

"I had him set up the tray on the ground beside me. There were two plates. The food was essentially the same; only the more careful garnishments identified mine, while the larger portions distinguished Sven's. He must have had substantial dietary needs for his workouts.

"He watched as I began to eat and stared, immobile, since I hadn't given him permission. Our meal was made up of cold sausages, various salads, and a selection of fresh fruits that was so generous its size had to be at least partially for the visual effect.

"I ate the food with my fingers. Occassionally, I would take part of it and offer it to him. He would lean forward and eat from my hand, carefully licking it clean after every serving I gave him.

"I kept that up for a while and then altered my method. I put small piles of salads on parts of my body and would nod to him to give him permission to lick it up off my stomach, my chest or my thigh. The game had potential. There's no need for prudish behavior on such a private island. I eventually pushed down my trunks and had Sven carefully using his mouth to pull pieces of food out of my pubic hair.

"When we had both eaten as much as we wanted I indulged myself further. Sven took away our plates and brought me more wine. I sat there and had him do a series of poses for me, just those that a body-builder might use in a competition. It was ... amusing."

"Didn't you ever just have sex with him?" Tim asked.

"Of course ... That afternoon, in fact. After I was satisfied with my viewing, I had him go and get a condom for us. When he came back I had him put it on me. He was still well lubricated from the dildo and I had him squat on my cock just has he had done on the rubber contraption. He seemed to appreciate it much more.

"From then on, Sven became my constant companion. The professor had witnessed some of my activities and that night, at dinner, suggested that I continue them for the duration of my stay. He had already ordered that Sven's dinner be delayed until I decided whether or not I wanted to feed him myself.

"The professor and I understood that Sven was getting something fairly rare out of my attentions and we both knew that he would benefit from them."

"How can you say that?" Marc demanded.

"Sven is huge..."

"How big is he?" Tim asked.

"He is probably six feet and three inches tall. He weighs at least two hundred and fifty pounds. He has the hair and the demeanor of a warrior, as I said. That was for the benefit of the other slaves. But there are so many other masters that the professor and I knew who would have seen Sven and who wouldn't have been able to fight off the temptation of switching roles with him. Given that kind of build, they would..."

"They'd want to jump on his cock and make believe he was their master," Marc delivered his analysis with open contempt. I couldn't argue with his judgment.

"Yes. It's a problem that many, many large slaves have. It becomes difficult for them to find a master who can really take control of them and do it with any honest desire. The professor certainly wasn't one of those. But he had four other slaves to see to and he was getting on in years. I, however, was there at that moment and delighting in giving Sven a lesson in his position."

"You probably rode him like a horse," Marc snorted.

"No. Unfortunately the island was too small and there weren't any trails. It would have been very amusing to hitch him up to some kind of cart or carriage. I would have enjoyed it. But that wasn't possible. I did swim with him once though and I did grab hold of his powerful shoulders and have him carry me through the water. It was a singular experience to feel the strength of him and to know that it was supporting me in that way.

"Actually, most of our activities were very quiet and not at all melodramatic. Just as there would have been masters who couldn't control their occasional desire to be a slave, at least in the sense of momentary sexual pleasure, there would be others who would have seen Sven and would have had the professor's permission to deliver very severe punishments to him. Sven didn't really need those.

"He needed more subtle things. He moved a sleeping pad into my room that night. For the rest of my stay he slept on the floor at the bottom of my bed. He'd jump up in the morning and bring me my coffee, wearing only the small piece of white fabric held in place by the strings. He'd wait cautiously until I'd give him some kind of indication that he might perform some other service for me.

"I would often have him slip a condom on my cock and then suck on it, carefully holding his mammoth body on the points of his hands and feet so he didn't disturb the rest of me. Sometimes I would fuck him instead. I would have him on his stomach and have him lift up his midsection to expose his now hairless anus. I would thrust in and find myself supported by the small mountain of muscle that was mine for this week-long visit.

"I would sometimes allow him to orgasm as well, but seldom in the morning. It was much better to leave him in need during the day. When I did decide to allow him an orgasm in the evening, he'd truly apprciate my gift.

"Sven — big, powerful Sven — was able to display the deep yearnings he had for service. He wasn't at all ashamed to have changed from his leather; he seemed to grow quite fond of the g-string. He would see to my bath; he'd rub me dry with a huge towel afterwards; he would deliver all my meals and wait obediently until I was ready to feed him."

"And then you let him fuck you."

I stared at Marc, "You think that I'm one of the masters who desired to change roles with Sven? Hardly, Marc, hardly. I usually would let him come to where I was sitting late at night, perhaps in the living room in front of the fire where we would be with the professor and the other slaves. The big chairs that the professor had would help me support Sven's weight. I'd have him sprawl across my lap, hanging his legs off one arm of the chair and resting his back against the other. As big men often are, Sven was aware of the burden of his size and compensated for it quite well.

"Then I would tease him. I'd play with his cock, fondle his balls, perhaps pinch his tits. The others seemed to enjoy it a lot. I once had Benjamin come over and I humiliated Sven tremendou ly by having the other slave tell me what he thought that Sven really liked.

"When he said that Sven's pierced nipples were the center of his sexual response, I had Benjamin suck on first one, then the other in succession. I had the slave keep it up until there was a thick ribbon of precome flowing from Sven's cock-head to prove his arousal.

"In that case, and most others, I would finally masturbate Sven myself, whispering into his ears and letting him nuzzle his bearded face against me while his enormous arms wrapped around my neck. While I was talking he would cover my face with his kisses, much like an adoring feline.

"The professor used to have the other slaves play at sex for his amusement in the evening. Often our nights in front of the fire were spent watching them as he had them masturbate themselves or one of the others. He would sometimes set up a card game where the winner would be able to perform any act of choice on one of the other players. When that particular game was played one night, I offered Sven as their prize. They played endless hands of cards and I let them take Sven and put him in any position the winner chose, so long as they didn't orgasm. By the end of that evening all of them, Sven and the four others, were putty in our hands. When we finally told the four that they could come by rubbing against one another we were rewarded with the sight of a mass of handsome young male flesh squirming together, sending off the most powerful odors and finally ending up with a great sticky mess on the floor.

"I hadn't allowed Sven to join. Instead I took him to the bedroom and told him he might be given an orgasm only if he would plead earnestly enough. I'm not often turned on by the simple sound of another man's voice, but that night Sven was able to come up with some very erotic messages, indeed. And I allowed him to come eventually by having him put my cock inside his foreskin. I fucked the loose flesh and eventually drove him to his release by the rubbing together of our cockheads.

"I was pleased to see when I left that two of the professor's problem slaves had been well taken care of. Daniel was as subservient as possible. He still had bruises from his punishment a week afterward. He had resumed his role as well-trained slave.

"When he had the other four row me to the mainland, Sven put on his long pants and his shirt once more. I had noticed that he had brought his leather outfit to the dock and left it there. After he returned he was going to go back to his former overseer self.

"He seemed sad as he called out the cadence to the oarsman. He looked at me whenever he could, whenever he dared. When the boat got to the pier and we had climbed out we stood and stared at one another for a while. He cried and then, carefully telling me that the professor had allowed it, he gave me a few small gifts."

"How touching," Marc said disdainfully.

"Yes, it was. But, now, I'm afraid it's late and this will have to be the end of our story-telling. You two have had quite a bit to drink." I picked up the nearly empty bottle they had both been pouring from. "I don't think you should drive home. Stay here tonight."

"So you can sneak into our room and shackle us, take us off and sell us to some Arabian sheik?"

"Marc, you know better than that. You've been coming to this house for years now and you've never even had a pair of handcuffs put on you. It is late; you have been drinking; neither of you work tomorrow. Stay. Tomorrow you can swim in the pond and lay in the sun."

I think Marc might have argued about it; he was not in a very friendly mood. But when he stood up he stumbled and his tipsy condition was all too apparent. He shrugged and Tim said, "Sure, you're right."

I put them in separate bedrooms and then went to my own suite. I undressed and climbed into the covers. Marc had actually been correct. I did have a motive in their staying the night in my house. This was perfect, I thought. The two of them wouldn't be able to escape the thoughts and dreams that I would have invoked with my tales. They would both be in bed now; remembering the descriptions and wondering what things had really been like. They were both probably masturbating on my clean sheets; they would have to be thinking that I was so close by. When they woke up, the memory of these dreams would still be there and they would find me waiting. They would have to deal with my reality. I drifted off with a smile on my face.

A Confession

Tim was the first one to come downstairs the next morning. His eyes were still sleepy and his hair was mussed. He gratefully took a cup of coffee. I knew Tim was, actually, the more realistic possibility for my plans. At least he had more experience with my . . . areas of interest according to the stories I'd heard from Marc.

I realized that I had never heard of any of them from Tim's own mouth though. This morning conversation could be my opportunity for doing just that. I took my own coffee over to the table and sat down. I was trying to form the words to begin when Tim started himself.

"I know what you're doing," he said in a casual tone.

"And what, precisely, am I doing?"

"With these stories you're telling us all the time. You think that we're going to buy them, that you're going to be able to use them to get us into all that stuff."

"And just how do you know so much about 'all that stuff?'" I asked, intrigued by how far he might be willing to go.

My challenge obviously took him back a bit. He studied the coffee cup that was sitting in front of him on the table now. I wasn't about to let my advantage slip. "Marc's told me a few things about you and your biker friends."

My little statement had quite an effect. Tim's two hands gripped the cup. I could see the tension in his forearms as he clenched his muscles with anger. "He shouldn't have done that."

"He was only telling a friend something interesting about another friend. We lose control of words once they've been spoken to another. The ancients understood that. When you've begun to tell your tales to someone else, then they enter the mythology."

Tim wouldn't look up. He wouldn't even talk for a full minute. Finally, he lifted his eyes to meet mine. "That's how I know what you're doing and why. I know about you and your kind."

"I've already told you, Marc has only given me a few ideas of what happened to you. Certainly you don't seem the worse for wear. I would gamble that you're a better person for it all. How long ago was it? Two years."

"No. It was longer than that. I was just a kid."

"How old were you?"

"Eighteen, something like that."

"Seven years ago?"

"Yes. I'd just gotten out of high school then." He drank some more of his coffee and looked out the kitchen window to the lawn.

"So?" I was using all of my strength to keep my voice calm and not appear too anxious.

He finally began and I leaned forward with anticipation.

"You know that big motorcycle run they always have over in Laconia? The national thing where all the clubs from all over the country come? There are thousands of them in that little resort town every year. There have been some raunchy times, then there were some other years where everything was so family-oriented it might as well have been a Rotary convention."

"That was after they had to call in the National Guard because the bikers were tearing apart the place."

"Yeah, well, this was one of the last years that the thing was real — where it was a real biker thing and not all cleaned up for the sake of image and that kind of crap.

"I used to go over there every year to see what was going on. The bikers were sort of heroes to me; I used to think that I'd like to grow up and be just like them, outlaws on the road.

"This one time — after I'd graduated from high school and thought I was a tough guy — I went over to Laconia. I was just standing there wearing a t-shirt and a pair of cut-offs. This one big biker came over to me and smiled. That's all he did at first, he just smiled. It was frightening when he did it. He was a lot taller than I was — a lot more than six feet — and he was wearing really filthy clothes: dirty jeans and a leather jacket without a shirt. He wasn't really fat, but he was big and he had a belly on him. It looked like it was very firm — I know now that it was.

"He just waited for me to say something or move away or respond and all he did was smile down at me. I should have been smart enough to understand that just trying to escape was the best idea. But I thought I could deal with him." Tim shook his head as he remembered that obviously foolish moment.

"So, I finally said, 'Hi.' As soon as I did, he reached over and put a hand on my shoulder. I thought that was really cool, I mean, here was this big biker and he was acting as though I was a real pal, a buddy. He sort of rocked me back and forth with that hand.

"Then he said, 'You suck cock?' I couldn't believe it. I mean, yeah, I did. I'd been fooling around with the guys in school for years. But I was freaked that this guy could spot me in the middle of all these people and walk up and ask me if I . . . did it.

"I told him, 'Fuck no.' He just shrugged and took that big, warm hand of his off my shoulder. 'Too bad,' he said, 'you should learn how.'

"Then I did the most stupid thing of all." He had both hands back on his cup again. I waited, but he didn't seem to dare continue. A frown was building on his brow. I almost broke in and said something, but he began on his own:

"People talk about their big moments, the times when they make decisions that change everything, their whole lives. I made my own then. He was walking away from me and I called out, 'Come back.'

"He turned around and that smile was on his face again. He walked over to me and put both hands on my shoulders this time. I was biting my lip, I remember that. Finally, I said, 'Yeah, I do.'

"'You suck cock?' he said.

"'Yeah.' That's all I could say. He put an arm around my shoulder — it was huge, mammoth — and starting walking me away with him. I felt like my insides were going to explode with a weird mix of fear and excitement. I was just letting this biker take me away and I didn't know where we were going.

"We finally got to where his big Harley was parked. He got on and I started to get on behind him. But he stopped me. 'My holes sit in front,' he said, and he patted the seat in front of him. I didn't really know what he meant by 'hole,' in fact, I thought I misunderstood the word. But I didn't want to look stupid, so I didn't say anything. I lifted up my leg and straddled the Harley. He put his arms around me to get to the handlebars. I was enveloped in this big mass of a man who had all these odors.

"Some of them were just disgusting. I knew there was old piss. Some were just from the machine — oil and gasoline that had gotten into his clothes. But a lot of them were wonderful — sweat and . . . stuff.

"We went on then, back to where they were staying, the club he belonged to. It was back in the hills above Laconia, on a small lake. It was really quiet, far from the crowds.

"Somehow they'd gotten this place that was a collection of cabins. There were four of them, I think. Like a compound of sorts. They were close to one another, but you couldn't see any other building anywhere close by. It was totally private. Just as well . . . there were lots of things that went on that other people shouldn't see, lots of things."

He was remembering more and more details. I could see it in his face. I didn't want this story to end. I wanted to give him time to remember as many things as possible. I got up and poured more coffee for both of us and then sat back down to wait.

"What else?" I finally asked.

"What else." He leaned back in his chair and looked away again. "Stuff you — people like you would really like. I bet you'd like my story just as much as you like your own.

"We got there on his bike. When he got off, I started to follow. But first he reached down and he said, 'I don't like this shit.' Before I could do anything, he ripped off my shirt. He just put both hands on the back of my collar and he tore it off my back. 'Better,' was all he said. Then he started to walk away.

"I was sitting there with just some rags hanging on to my waist. I got rid of them and jumped off the bike to follow him.

"There was a whole group of people sitting around and smoking dope and drinking beer near the shore of the lake. I couldn't believe them. There were at least fifty men and women. Lots of the men were dressed like this guy I had driven out with. I heard them call him Steamer, that was his name. They had on leather and denim and boots. A few others were either swimming — mainly in the nude — or else they just had on shorts. Almost all the women had their tits hanging out, they didn't wear any blouses.

"I didn't know what it all meant yet. I'd learn that soon enough. Steamer flopped down on the ground next to one of his pals and told me to go and get us both a can of beer from the ice-filled barrel that was on the edge of the group. I thought that was cool; my buddy had brought me back to meet his friends and then wanted us to have a beer together. I wasn't paying attention to the way he'd made me admit I was a cock-sucker and the way he'd torn off my shirt.

"I just went and got it. 'Faster next time,' was the only thanks he gave me. I sat beside him and opened my own can. I figured he was just like me, that he was going to be really cool about being gay. These guys didn't seem that way and I thought that Steamer and I would probably sneak off later and have fun, but that we'd have to act real butch in front of these others.

"But, instead, he put his arm around me and dragged me up close to him. His hands ran over my bare chest. No, I can't say that. They weren't hands. They were paws. These big paws were feeling up my chest.

"'I got me a new hole,' he said to his friend who just laughed. 'Always had a weakness for boy-hole, don't you Steamer?' the other guy said. 'Sure do, sure do,' he answered. Then, in front of all those straight people, he reached down and put his hand on my pants over my cock and balls. I couldn't move. It was part being paralyzed by being scared of him and part that all these people were watching.

"But no one cared. I couldn't get over that. I was just sitting there and he was feeling me up and they just kept on drinking their beer. I liked it, all of a sudden, I just liked it. The biker with his smelly clothes and the touch of him holding me in public became more exciting and less frightening somehow.

"So I relaxed. I just decided to try to figure out who these strangers were. There were some of the women who were doing most of the work, I could tell that. They all were bare-breasted. They were getting the beers and some of them were starting to pile up wood at a spot where there'd obviously been a fire the night before. It was for food, I supposed.

"I didn't realize it then, but there were a couple men who were doing the same thing. It didn't sink in that they didn't have many clothes on either.

"All around were the club members, laughing and drinking and having a good time. There were lots of them who were feeling up women right in the open, just like Steamer was touching me. These guys would grab the women's tits and pull them onto their laps and suck on them, or else grab a chunk of ass or even their cunts.

"I got all excited watching it. Sex didn't happen this way where I grew up; that was for sure. Then this one woman who had long, long beautiful black hair was walking by a guy who reached up and got a hold of her leg and dragged her down beside him. She didn't seem to resist at all when he pulled down her jeans. There wasn't anything on underneath. He lifted her up in a funny way — with his arms under her ass — and then he leaned over and started to eat her out.

"She really got into it, yelling — not angry, turned on. The people around her just laughed more and talked to her and to the guy, egging them on. I got hard watching it all. Not because a woman would get me hard, but just seeing this sex in the outdoors without any restrictions.

"That's when I started to learn what a 'boy-hole' was. Steamer took the back of my neck and he pushed me — hard — down onto his smelly crotch. He used his other hand to pull out his erection and then he shoved again. There wasn't any doubt what I was supposed to do. There was also no way I was going to escape that beefy hand on the back of my neck.

"I was all turned on again, just with the idea that these people were watching me. Someone yelled something to me, I never heard what it was, but it wasn't a real put-down, it was more like an encouragement.

"For some reason I decided I was going to be good at it — really good. I got it into my head that I wanted Steamer to be proud of me. I sucked that big smelly cock of his like it was the last lollipop on earth.

"I went at it for a long time, I lost track of how long. Then he lifted me up off it. I was ... I felt like some kind of sex maniac, I guess. I had spit rolling down my chin and his cock was still standing up straight into the air. I dove down, to get it back again.

"That really made him happy and he laughed at that, so did the guy beside him, but he wouldn't let me have it, 'No, little boy-hole, don't get greedy.'

"We just sat for a while and drank some beer. More and more people were starting to have sex. One other guy was going down on another man. That was the first time I happened to notice that he was one of the ones who wasn't wearing a shirt.

"Steamer had gone on and on, telling me how much he liked my body — this is before all my chest hair grew out." Tim reached down and absent-mindedly played with some of the thick growth that was on his forearm now, as though it was incongruous with the memory of his past that was flooding out of him. He stopped and went back to his story.

"He told this guy beside him that he liked boy-holes with no hair. That we were better fucks than women. 'Girl-holes and boy-holes are all the same,' he said, 'except a boy-hole's brown and a girl-hole's pink. Of course, all you gotta do is slap the boy-hole's bottom around a little bit and it'll be pink, too.'

"They both thought that was really funny and laughed a lot about it. I was embarrassed, really embarrassed. But it was hardly the time to make protests, not after I'd sucked him off in front of everyone else.

"It kept on going like that for hours. Sex all around us and some of those bare-breasted women fixing a barbecue dinner over this enormous fire. Things got much more intense, but the buzz from the beer made it all seem okay. I wasn't used to drinking that much, and I couldn't hold it well.

"I just had these fuzzy memories of Steamer and me making out and him putting his hands down my pants and finally taking them off. When the food was ready and put out on a picnic table, Steamer told me to go and get a couple plates for us. I didn't mind; it didn't seem like a big deal; so I did it.

"Later on, he pulled out a joint and we smoked it. I got really buzzed then. There were a lot of things that happened that night that I couldn't remember, even the next morning. I woke up in a sleeping bag with Steamer. His big body was all wrapped around mine. My nipples were very sore, I did remember that he'd chewed on them a lot. So was my ass where he'd fucked me — and slapped me around a bit.

"I was sort of dazed. I got up out of the sleeping bag and was going to go to the lake to swim and see if that would clear my head. My movements must of woken up Steamer. He grabbed me and pulled me back into the bag. I didn't want to get fucked again, not the way my ass felt. But I couldn't fight him at all, he was too big. He started to move his cock inside me and I just cried and begged him to stop.

"It wasn't me that changed his mind. 'Why the hell are you dried up in there? Where's your grease?' I didn't know what to think. He got up and — with his hard cock standing straight in the air like some angry red battering ram — he went and got a bottle of lubricant.

"He brought it back to where I was still laying half in and half out of the sleeping bag. He threw it at me hard. I remember that it hurt a lot and I knew at once that there'd be a bad bruise on my hip where it had landed.

"'Grease up your hole,' he said. I was petrified. It had been one thing when he was trying to fuck me and I was sore; it was something else when he purposely hurt me with the bottle. Thank god I had enough sense not to fight him. I opened the bottle and put a smear of grease up my ass, trying to ignore the giggles from the people who were close enough to know what was going on.

"Then Steamer got back in the sleeping bag with me and started to fuck me. It wasn't as bad with the lubricant, though I was still very sore. I was just there, not fighting him, maybe not even totally conscious of what was going on.

"When he was done, he pulled out and rolled over. In a couple minutes he was snoring again. I did crawl out this time and pulled on my cut-offs. I was too shaky from the beer and dope to get it together to just leave; the idea of a swim in the lake was getting stronger. I walked to the shore and put my feet in the water. It felt wonderful. I got out of my shorts and dove in.

"When I came back to shore there was a guy waiting for me. He was very handsome. He was older than I was, I guess he was about twenty-five. He had dark hair and a great smile. He was only wearing a pair of cut-off jeans and boots. He had his hands on his waist and a big smile.

"He was as tall as Steamer, maybe, but much trimmer. That's only in relationship to Steamer's big belly, though. He was muscular compared to anyone else. And his chest was covered with hair. He looked really hot.

"He handed me a towel when I got out of the water. 'I haven't had a chance to say hello to you,' he said. He told me his name was Howie and he was one of the club members. I immediately assumed that he was putting the make on me. I said something about it — about being scared that Steamer wouldn't like it — and he thought that was really funny.

" 'I'm a hole, too,' he said. Then I finally got it explained to me, the things about the club. I was pretty upset. That word — 'hole' — wasn't just something that Steamer was saying. It was a word they all used. They were all divided into two groups: holes and tops. Most of the holes were women, but not all; and the opposite with tops."

"There were female tops in the bike club?" I was sure that couldn't be.

"Oh, yes, there were. Most of them were lesbians. But I saw ... Some of the tops were women. Howie explained it all to me while we were sitting on the shore, letting the sun dry me off from my swim. I wanted to say that it was disgusting and leave, but I was naked and my cock was hard while he told me what the rules of the place were.

"Every hole was there for every top. You had a 'main top' most of the time and so long as you were with that top, the rest of them would respect it and leave you alone. But when a top told you to do something, you did it. 'And fast,' Howie said.

"When I pressed him about it, he got strange and just said that the club didn't like it when holes got out of line. If you wanted to stay with the club, then you did what they said when they said it.

"I couldn't understand why this big stud was a hole. I was already assuming that it was a bad thing to be. I asked him about that. He just shrugged. He said, 'Let me tell you something. There are two kinds of people in this world that it's worth being: Tops and holes. You are what you are and if you're lucky enough to be one of them, you're thankful. Anything else is just too boring.'

"I told him I thought that was strange. I wasn't so sure about this stuff. To tell you the truth, if I hadn't been so uptight about being cool the way teenagers are, I think I would have broken down and cried. It was all too bizarre. Howie told me not to worry, to just go with it. He was like you." Tim looked at me closely, as though he wanted to make sure that I understood something. "He just thought you should do it well. And that you should take something like that as an opportunity to experience more than other people will ever know about.

"He gave me some pointers, though they weren't exactly encouraging, to me at least. I asked him how males could be holes. I was worried about that. He said I shouldn't be. Howie's explanation was simple: Males just had to work harder at it. Women were at an advantage because they had three places for a top to work on, a man only had two. We just had to learn to use the two we had — our mouths and our assholes — better than the females. It was like the female tops, he said, who had to become more creative since they only had their hands and their mouths while the men tops had cocks besides. He told me that women holes always got off on women tops because they had taught themselves so well how to use what they had. We had to do the same thing.

"He also said I should make sure that Steamer was happy with me in all ways, not just my mouth and ass, though those were very important. If Steamer was happy, then he'd keep me close by and I wouldn't have to worry about the rest of them. How was I supposed to do that, I wondered. He told me his tricks, that I was always to try to crawl in between Steamer's legs, for one thing. 'Tops like it when there's a face near their crotches,' was his simple explanation.

"But whatever I did, he warned me, I had to follow every order and do it fast. 'Don't aggravate them, ever. If they want sex, give it to them. If they want a can of beer, run to get it. If you don't, you'll find out how mean this group can be.'

"We talked for maybe a half hour about all of this stuff, these ideas and roles that were so alien to me. Then Howie decided we should lighten it up. We went back into the water and fooled around a little bit. We sat back in the sun; this time both of us had to dry off.

"Howie told me about himself and his main top, a guy named Torch. I couldn't get over the story. They weren't always like this. There was a time when Howie thought he had to be a bad dude and he and Torch used to prowl the bars and alleys in Detroit, where they lived. They did all kinds of shit together as buddies. But Howie knew that he was in love with Torch all along. But the way he was in love didn't have anything to do with the way that Howie could see other people doing it. He certainly didn't see other men acting the way he felt, so he hid it.

"Then they met Steamer. It turns out that Steamer's really the founder of the club. It was just getting started back then. Steamer came and talked to Howie and Torch about it, he wanted them to join. He explained that there had to be certain firm rules about the way people acted. He was the one who demanded that men and women could switch roles, that they could be whatever their nature led them to be. And he was the one who said that the ones who were on the bottom — the ones they'd eventually call 'holes' — had to belong to everyone.

"By the time Steamer was done giving his pitch, Torch was all set to go. Howie was too, but he had to wait till later that night to explain to Torch just what that meant for him. They'd been together ever since.

"Somehow, Howie's story made me feel much better. I was able to focus on what had been exciting about Steamer and being in the camp and not on what was scaring me, that's the best way to put it. I felt like he understood and if a guy like him could get off on the things that I had seen and done, well, then it was okay.

"There was something else about Howie. No one had ever talked to me so honestly before. I'd responded and been truthful with him. We knew each other's secrets in just a few minutes, it seemed. It scared me, that someone knew things about me, but I was also really happy that I could tell him things and he wouldn't think I was weird. He accepted me. He kept touching me, not really sexually, but like he was letting me know that things were all right by putting a hand on my belly or on my head if he thought I needed a little support. In that short time, I think he became closer to me than any other man I'd ever known. And we shared something together besides. Even if it was just being holes, we were the same kind of person. That made me feel just great.

"We got ready to go back to the camp. We were taking this short path. There were some people not far from where we'd been sunning ourselves. Howie and I were still carrying our shorts and shoes. We were naked, which I could tell was okay in the club area, and that it was especially all right for the holes. I was already thinking about myself that way: As one of the holes like Howie.

"We came on these two guys, tops. They were standing up with their pants down by their knees. In front of them were these two naked women. The women were having a real hard time of it. The men were yelling at them, calling them really filthy names. They were pawing the women's breasts in a way that was obviously causing them a lot of pain. The tops were saying that the women were lousy cocksuckers.

"These two girls were crying. I was back to being petrified, especially once the tops saw Howie and me. One of them pulled his woman's face away from his cock and threw her aside with this sneer. He had a stumpy cock, but it was fat, really wide and thick. He had big balls. He shook his cock and he was staring at me. 'Boyholes know about cocksucking.'

"I froze. But I felt Howie's hand on the small of my back, nudging me forward. He'd told me over and over again not to hesitate when one of them wanted something. So I moved ahead towards the guy and knelt down in front of him.

"Just as I did, I heard the other top saying that his pal was right. They shouldn't bother with women that didn't know how to use their mouths. I knew what he was doing. He was motioning to Howie to come over and suck him off. I already had the fat cock down my throat and my face was stuck in the smelly pubic hair of the guy I was sucking. Then I could sense Howie beside me.

"It was the most intense moment in my life, having him doing that at the same time, especially when he reached over and took my hand. We sucked off the two tops together, and it was . . . magical. They didn't even exist for me, it was just me and Howie.

"When they were done — and they told us we really were better than the women — Howie and I were left alone again. I didn't have to say anything, we just embraced and rolled onto the grass. We just stayed there for a long time, with our arms around each other and our hard cocks pressing up against one another's bellies.

I don't think I've ever had such a perfect moment with another human being, not ever."

"You haven't experienced that with Marc?"

He looked at me with complete disbelief, he must have understood what I was really saying, that he could try. I was surprised that he was willing to be honest with me. "No, I haven't had anything close to that with Marc."

I was even more pleased when he went on. He must have decided that so much had been said that there was no reason not to continue. There were few secrets left.

"I think I would have stayed just for Howie. So long as there was even a chance that I could have that moment with him again, I would have gambled anything to try. He was like a big brother, I suppose. He liked me a lot. He told me I was like him in many ways. He was happy for me, he said I was really getting into it, that he could tell I was, and that he liked seeing someone understand where he should be at an early age, not wait too long.

"We did all kinds of things. It was easy because Torch and Steamer were good buddies and it was simple to arrange for the four of us to be near each other. It wasn't bad, not at all. Steamer thought it was wonderful that I was learning things so early and he liked the way that Howie would watch over me. Like, making sure that I greased up my ass. That was the one thing about men that Steamer didn't like, that you had to grease them up to fuck them. He thought that boy-holes should always be ready. It insulted him that the place he wanted to fuck was too dry.

"Torch was the same way. So he made Howie do it too. Every morning, first thing, Howie and I would take the lubricant and put it up our asses for the tops. It was as automatic as anything else. And when we'd be together during the day, we'd check each other, putting our fingers up our asses to make sure the tops could get in easy if they wanted to.

"There were other things that Steamer liked about me. I had taken Howie's lesson well and kept my face as close to Steamer's crotch as I could. I was always ready for him.

"One day, only the third or fourth that I was in the camp, Steamer took me to this guy who did leather work and had some stuff made for me. There was a pair of shorts that he wanted me to wear. They had zippers up the front, just like you'd expect, but there was also one up the rear so he could just pull the one tab and be able to get into me.

"Things went on. I thought this was the best place I'd ever been, with this biker who liked me and Howie, the best friend I'd ever known. It was pretty wonderful. But I couldn't escape the way there was so much possibility of violence in the camp. You could sense it, like it was a physical force all itself.

"And there were plenty of actual violent things that happened. All of a sudden there'd be a scream and you'd see some hole getting it from some top with a belt, or being kicked or something. No one ever, ever tried to stop it or cool the top down. There were other things too. I'd feel very good about Steamer and Howie and Torch, but there'd suddenly be some top who'd come along while I was walking to get a beer, or take a dip in the lake, and he'd just tell me to suck him, or else to fall on the ground and spread my legs.

"They wouldn't simply fuck you. There was more to it. You'd have to lift your ass up in the air with your knees spread far apart. Sometimes they'd want to slap your ass — they'd call that 'warming you up.' You were never safe from them, from the sudden interference of someone you had no right to talk back to or say no to. The vulnerability was total.

"There was one night that was the worst of all. The tops were mainly straight, like I said. They used to think that it was, well, cute that there were male holes — and they'd get blow jobs from us and stuff. But they really were the usual straight bikers you think about and the way that guys like me and Howie were treated was different than they would have done it, themselves, at least for the most part. It was just because Steamer liked men and Torch loved Howie and they were in on the beginning of the club that it was so loose about sex things. Once that began to happen, then they also attracted some of these very scary women tops and a few other gay and bi guys who weren't welcome in most other clubs.

"This one night, the regular bikers and the women tops decided they'd have some fun with the women holes. They wanted to see them wrestle. They wanted it to be just like in the sleazy nightclubs — they wanted them to mud wrestle. Howie and I and a couple of the other male holes had to make a mud puddle for them.

"Everyone was pretty loaded on beer and dope and having a

good time. These girls would get in the pit we'd dug and they'd have to wrestle one another. It was. . ."

I couldn't believe that Tim stopped so suddenly. After all he'd said, this one memory was clearly the most horrible. I wondered about it for a moment, and then I understood. "It was the opposite of what you'd had with Howie."

"Yes, that was it. They were forcing the women to fight against one another when the only strength they had was from one another. It was terrifying — not just scary, but terrifying — to think that you'd have to be totally alone as a hole and have to fight another hole. I shivered, I actually shivered. . .

"My worst fear came true. Steamer was getting really rowdy. After we watched these obscene fights with the women holes pulling off each others' clothes and shoving one another's face into the mud, Steamer got it into his mind that some boy-holes should do the same thing. He shoved me forward and challenged any other top to send another boy-hole in with me for the big event.

"Thank god that Torch wasn't right there at the moment. I was looking at Howie and we were both just horrified that maybe we'd have to fight each other. I couldn't have done that, I know I couldn't have. . ."

"Of course you would have," I said.

He grit his teeth with anger when he heard me saying that. "I don't know," he admitted. "But I didn't have to find out. It was bad enough as it was. There was a bi guy named Boot. He was a hole for a woman top named Elsa — they were one of the only such combinations in the camp. I had watched the two of them together and I sure didn't envy him his place.

"I used to watch when they'd have sex. Almost always Elsa would have him eat her out. Every time you saw them it seemed like he was on his knees between her legs. But sometimes she wanted to fuck. He'd have to spread eagle on the ground just the way we did, but face up. He couldn't touch her, that was her rule. She straddle him and he'd have to stay in that one position the whole time. She called it 'riding' him, and it was a pretty authentic description.

"It was incredible to watch the women tops, by the way. They seemed to want to make sure that they were tougher than the males; they didn't want to be underestimated. They were far more vicious to the women holes and they were the worst to the boy-holes. Boot even had to have his nipples pierced for Elsa and he had a permanent metal collar around his neck. He must have liked it — he never tried to leave — but it certainly looked like the worst existence in the camp.

"Anyway, Elsa pushed Boot out. He was much bigger than me, and older. Probably about twenty-seven or eight. He was laughing and high and having a good time. It didn't bother him and the crowd loved having the two of us in there together.

"Steamer thought having two males there called for a special touch. He didn't want us fighting in the mud. He brought out cans of motor oil. He had the two of us strip naked and then he poured the oil over our bodies, in our hair, gallons of it.

"I was stupid enough to think that Boot wouldn't really mean it. I thought he had to be like me and Howie and that he'd understand that we shouldn't do anything to each other." Tim shook his head as he recalled how very wrong he had been.

"We started in, with the crowds yelling at us. Boot and I couldn't get a hold on each other. The oil made our skin too slippery and we'd fall every time we tried to make a move. But, after a while, Boot got me from behind. He got his arms underneath mine and reached both of them up until he could get a grip on my neck. That was it, I thought, he'd won.

"I hadn't really tried. I just wanted the humiliation to be over and to stop thinking about what it meant for us to be fighting one another. Maybe the crowd knew I hadn't fought well, maybe it was assumed all along. . .

"I could feel Boot's cock getting hard against the crack of my ass. Even if I hadn't greased myself up before, there was so much oil over all of us that it wouldn't have made any difference. Even while we were standing like that — with me immobile — he was able to throw me down.

"Everyone thought that was great and there was all this applause and all these obscene things being said. I was crying — that only made them happier — and Boot got harder and fucked me harder in front of everyone. They especially liked it when I got hard myself. I couldn't help it.

"I was just mortified, I was more than embarrassed, and I was scared. I was really scared. This was the first time the violence of the place had honestly been directed at me.

"When Boot finally let me go, all I could do was think about Howie's advice that I should always stay between Steamer's knees so I would be protected. I didn't even stand up, still on all fours, I moved towards Steamer as fast as I could. I got to him and I opened his pants and brought out his cock. He loved it. He was laughing and carrying on about what a hungry boy-hole I was.

"Even so, the show had turned on another top. I could feel him moving up behind me. 'No.' I thought, 'you can't have me while I'm sucking Steamer's cock.' I believed it was some rule. But it wasn't. It had only been advice. Even while I was there, sucking on Steamer, another guy was poking my ass and then he put his cock up there. I was on my knees, cock at both ends, crying, covered with oil.

"It didn't help at all when I finally had a chance to look beside me and see that the same thing was happening to Howie with Torch and someone else. Actually it made it worse, because I knew that the display I'd put on had gotten the tops all excited and led them to this small orgy."

"It could be done then," I said, remembering the past with my usual nostalgic regret.

"Yeah, back then it was still all right from that point of view, at least.

"The night ended and, I don't know how, but I got through it. Howie took me to the lake and helped me clean up. We talked a bit about things and how I felt. Then it was over.

"It really was all over about two weeks later. The club was going to move on. I hadn't even thought about plans. I wasn't living a real life, I was just there, immersed in the activities and the things I was learning about sex. But Steamer was a good guy. He was smart about a lot of things, I'd learn. He wasn't going to let me go with them. He told me I was too young and had to make too many decisions. I'd had the experience, that was enough.

"I was pretty upset. I knew that these weren't people who were going to be easy to find. They were hardly going to write post cards or letters and there was no permanent address for them. I was losing them.

"One day, Steamer took me for a ride. We used to go out on his Harley a lot. That was one of the reasons for the rear zipper. What Steamer liked to do is sit me on the saddle in front of him and unzip the rear. Then he'd pull out his cock and stuff it up me. The engine of the big Harley would vibrate so much that we could just sit there and get off that way, it was as though I had an electric dildo up me, constantly shaking my insides.

"When he drove the bike over the roads, it felt like I was getting a really, really rough fucking. It was an incredible sensation. And, since we were so close and it was all happening just between the zippered openings, we could ride through the middle of a town and no one would know that we were having sex right in front of them.

"Steamer put me on the bike that day and he undid the back of my pants. He got his cock out and shoved it up my hole, just the way he liked it. He took me to a place we'd been before. It was a smaller pond, a nice one, even more quiet than the one where the camp was. We both went swimming, which was very unusual. We both stripped down and dove in the water. We just played, like we were both kids. He even washed himself, I remember that, he brought soap and he lathered up and even shampooed his hair.

"Afterwards, we laid out in the sun. It was pleasant, nice. It was totally different than it usually was — he wasn't ordering me around and he wasn't moving to try to fuck me. We just talked about little things. I got very sad. I rolled over and put my head on his huge chest and I felt this sense of loss like I'd never had before.

"That moment with Howie wasn't my only special time with the club, I realized. There were things with Steamer that were important to me too. And I was going to lose them all. I was going back to being a kid in a small town and this was the end of it. I cried and Steamer didn't get mad at me the way he might have before. He just hugged me.

"We both started to get hard and I figured he'd fuck me now. But he didn't. He knelt between my legs and he took both our cocks in his hands and began to rub them together. It felt incredible, especially because he was doing it. It was as though this man who'd been so rough with me was finally saying that I was grown up somehow.

"He talked to me, gently, while he manipulated our cocks. He told me I was too young for the road yet. That I had to learn things. He told me that someday I'd find out things about myself that he'd already seen in me. When the time was right, he said, then I'd find out about a group of people called The Network."

"What?" I wasn't prepared for that sudden revelation.

"Yes," Tim said, looking me squarely in the eye, "He told me that I'd find The Network when the time was right and if it was meant to be. He had been a part of it — I don't know how, I didn't know enough to ask him.

"Then he kept on masturbating us until we both came. We washed off in the lake and . . . And that was it. I went home that evening. Steamer drove me close to my parents' house. I went back to the camp later in the week and they were gone. I never heard anything about them again. I'd just about stopped thinking about them and The Network until I met Marc and moved in with him. Then you. He told me about you and your strange stories. Now I've heard a lot of them. Now I remember what Steamer said about The Network and I'm scared, I'm terrified that it's real."

An Accusation

Marc came downstairs. I got him coffee and the three of us had an innocent conversation about the summer weather and the influx of tourists. It was obvious that they were going to avoid any serious discussion right now, at least as long as all three of us were sitting at the table together.

I had expected them to take up my offer to spend the day swimming in my pond. But they'd have none of it. A quick sense of discomfort settled in the kitchen when I mentioned it and they both stood and made excuses, claiming they'd each made other promises.

The rest of the day was consumed with the pleasant and easy tasks of living in the mountains in the summer. I made phone calls, did office work and then wandered around the expansive property. It felt like a baron's domain, though, in fact, the cost of real estate in this part of the country is so minimal that I had been able to purchase this extravagant privacy for little.

But I had plans for it. I wandered the perimeter of the cleared section of lawn and thought once more about pushing the heavy brush back further and having a more professional job done on the lawn which was too heavily composed of weeds.

I remembered Marc's comment about the wonders that could be achieved by slave labor. Yes, I smiled and told myself, it could be quite something. But I wasn't sure what the latest developments meant. They puzzled me. While it might seem that Tim's revelations about his time with the bikers and the top's prediction that he would eventually meet up with The Network would seem a very positive step, there was still the chance that things could go wrong.

I shouldn't have worried so much about that. Everything proceeded in a most remarkably beneficial manner. I heard a car come up my drive that night. I was sitting in my living room reading the latest in the remarkable Sleeping Beauty books and, as always, I was being swept away by the vision of elegant slavery that only A. N. Roquelaure can produce. There aren't that many people who would arrive at my house without forewarning, but it wasn't that strange, either, that a friend or neighbor would come by for some unannounced reason.

I went to the door and opened it just as Tim was about to ring my bell. "Come in."

"Thank you." He moved past me, almost slinking against the wall as though he wanted to avoid touching me. He went into the living room and stood in front of the fire I had lit to cut the evening chill. He put his hands out toward it, as though to warm them. I came back in the room after him and sat back in my chair.

I wouldn't speak. I refused to allow myself to ask why he had come to me. I wanted the confession to be given without any outside influence.

It took a while, but not too long, before he said anything. The beginning was just an awkward set of apologies, "I hope I'm not disturbing anything?"

"No, no. It's fine. I've done what work I had to finish today and was just entertaining myself with a book."

He tried to use that as an escape and came over to look at the cover. He picked the volume up off the table beside me. As soon as he read the full title — *Beauty's Punishment: The Further Erotic Adventures of Sleeping Beauty* — he dropped the volume as though it was a red-hot brick.

"You never leave it alone, do you? Everything about you is this."

"This? Sex? No, that's not true. There are many different books on the shelves in this room. Just take a look."

"I don't mean that. I mean . . . when you do anything with sex it's always this kind."

"Just about. Though I have been known to explore different experiences. And you?"

"Why are you asking me?" The tone of his voice was the answer to his own question. He was nervous, walking around on the balls of his feet, his head moving in quick jerks to scan the room as though he were afraid that someone might be listening in on this conversation.

"It interests me, that's all."

He moved back to the fire and stared at it again. It seemed to calm him down. His voice was more even when he spoke the next time. "Did you know Steamer? The guy I talked about? He said he had been in The Network — the same group you tell your stories about."

"No, at least I can't recognize him from your descriptions at all. You must remember that The Network — at least where I interact with it — is totally different than your biker club. Though I should have seen the similarities and I should have been more prepared for your revelation."

"Just what similarities are you talking about?"

"The fact that the gender of the person didn't dictate the role he or she took in that world. The way that there was so little absolute ownership of the slaves — the holes as they called them. That, you realize, isn't really for the sake of the tops. They would have been happy in any case. That was for the slaves, to make sure they lived in their constant state of understanding. Also, the fact they sent you away. That's hardly the usual response of an outlaw group to a young, handsome initiate.

"But how your Steamer knew about The Network? I don't know."

"Do you think he was a slave?" The question seemed to fascinate Tim.

"Perhaps. Or he might have been one who chose to move on and leave behind the structured world of moneyed elegance. That happens, and quite often. More and more, the masters of The Network see money as something useless other than for its utility in procuring slaves-for-purchase. The rewards of corporate life or vocational advancement aren't really very appealing to them. They choose to leave it all behind. Though they usually do that with their households intact.

"Steamer might have been a recruited slave when he was young. Or else, he might have entered The Network when he was a highly driven businessman, thinking he needed to expand the area of his control and dominance to include even his sexual life. Once there, he would have learned that it wasn't so. The idea of being the creator of a sexual bike club could certainly have appealed tremendously to a man who had seen the shallow rewards of business success."

"It wouldn't bother me if he had been a slave. He would have done it well, I bet. And he wouldn't have been ashamed of it."

"I'm sure not. No one would ever try to make him feel that way."

"I wish he had told me, though. I wish I had known from him what it had been like."

"Why?"

"Because then I could have loved him even more, even as much as I loved Howie."

"'Love' isn't the word I'd use to describe his feelings for you, not as you described them."

"Well, I told you a lot, but there were other things. When I was with him for those few weeks and he was trying to train me, I learned that he wasn't doing it to be cruel. He was doing it to help me. He wanted me to be the best there was. I told you about that first time when I decided that I was going to suck his cock really, really well. He picked up on that. It was one reason I got to stay as long as I did. He knew I was trying."

"He wanted you to be beautiful."

"Yes, that's it. Is it what you want from me?" He turned away from the flames and looked at me.

"Is it what you want me to give you?"

"I don't know." Tim moved over and sat on the couch opposite from my chair. "I just remember those weeks with the biker club and I remember everything that's come since and there's no comparison. None."

There was another car in the drive. "I wasn't expecting anyone," I said to Tim. I went back to the door. Of course, I should have expected it. Marc was storming up the walk. "Is he here?" He was speaking with barely controlled anger.

"Yes." There was no doubt who he meant and I didn't intend to lie.

Marc walked past me, into the living room. "Why are you

here? You said you were going to the inn."

"Why are *you* here? What right do you have to follow me?"

"I'm your lover."

The two of them stood in the living room. Marc's fists were clenched and his arms were strained with muscles dancing up and down their length. He made it appear as though all his self-control was necessary to keep himself from starting to swing.

Tim was more relaxed. He turned his back on Marc and looked at the fire again. "Lover? We've never used that word before." His voice was soft, almost seductive.

"Words! Who cares about words."

"I do," Tim responded with that same soft voice. He knelt down and put another piece of wood on the fire. "I care a lot. I care about the words we whisper to each other in the night. Haven't you ever wondered about that? Why it is that we both use the same words at night?"

"I don't know what you mean." But something had gotten to Marc. The fight was gone from his voice.

"Come on, think about it. Think about how unattached we are. 'Lovers?' Be serious. We're a couple guys who decided to live together so we could have a safe piece of cock every once in a while and not have to worry too much about it. 'Lovers?' We share the rent, we talk about jobs and school. We're a little bit supportive on bad days and we share a few of the good times. That's it. That's all.

"What's real is when we're in bed at night. What we say to each other under the covers. I can tell a lot from that. The way we each say the same things. And want the same things. Tell him about it."

Tim stood up now and looked directly into Marc's eyes as he continued. "Tell him how we are, when we're honest and the lights are out. Tell him how we get hard when we tell each other his stories and think about what he really wants from us. Tell him how, when you're getting ready to come, you beg me to bite your tits harder and harder. Or, how when you're jerking off and I have my arms around you, you ask me to grab hold of your balls and squeeze them. Or, how when you're getting close to coming you ask me to climb on top of you and straddle your belly so you can feel what it's like to have a man up there. Tell him."

"No." Marc's voice was almost hollow now. "No, I won't."

"Then I will. I'll tell him how every single honest expression of sexual desire that comes from us is bottom — hole — slave. That every time we're sincere, we let the words out about our fantasies. But that's only in bed. And that's why we never talk about being 'lovers,' because we aren't. The rest of our life together is just housekeeping and daily chores and having someone, anyone. It might be better than being alone, but not it's not as good as being happy and honest."

"What are you trying to do?" Marc demanded. "Are you trying to say that you really want those things he's always talking about? How can you?"

"Because I do. I always have. You do. I know you want them as badly as I want them. It's in your dirty talk and your dreams. It's in the magazines you read the most carefully and the television shows you insist on seeing. It's in the movies, even the books. And you even hide them from me — or you think you do. Here, look, I've seen this one before."

Tim went over and picked up the Roquelaure. He shoved it towards Marc. "Deny it. Deny that there's a well-read copy of this in the glove compartment of your car. I dare you to. Even though you'll sit and tell me how weird his stories are when we go out to dinner and even when you tell me that the bikers I was with were sick, you're driving out on country roads and jerking off to this. You love it. You want it. Maybe even as much as I do."

Marc physically moved back to avoid the verbal attack that his friend was delivering. "But that book is a fantasy. It's a story. Just a piece of fiction about some other time and place. It can't be real."

"You know that's not true. You know he's telling you about real things. I've told you about real things. Those bikers and Steamer's demands were real. It's there if we'll take it."

"It's sick to take it."

"Sicker than just thinking it?"

"Yes," Marc said adamantly. "You don't have to do everything you think."

"Maybe not. Of course not," Tim said. "But you don't have to take things the expected way either. You can reach out for the different ways, the new experiences. Look at us, look at us being two little faggots living together and thinking it's hot shit when we go to Boston and walk into a leather bar.

"And just why do we always go to leather bars when we go to the city, Marc? Why is that?" Tim's voice was picking up a sarcastic edge now. "Is that a little game of chicken? Huh? Do we go and see if there's something there that can make us do the things we'd only think about otherwise? Are we hoping that's what will happen? Why are we so very chicken that we won't go for the real thing when it's in front of us? Tell me that?"

Marc was on the defensive. He moved over to the couch and sat down. "We can't do everything we want. We have to make plans. That's why we want to go to college. That's why we agreed to go together, so we'd have a future."

"I don't want to spend the rest of my life thinking that I could have done something, that I had a chance. I've already spent years regretting the bikers. Now I have another opportunity. I know one of two things are going on: Either this is happening because it was meant to — the bikers were really only a preparation for this — or else, this is probably a grand mistake, the last time I'll even know about this world happening.

"I'm not going to take the chance that it's going to pass me by again, Marc. I'm not."

"What do you mean?" Marc was frightened now.

Tim turned to me. "Will you train me for The Network?"

"No!" Marc stood up and moved over to Tim. He put an arm around his shoulder. "You can't do it. You can't go into that. What about me?"

"What about you? Why don't you join me? Maybe we can be like me and Howie were — really share something. Not just washing dishes and going to bars and wishing, but doing things together that could never be forgotten. We could stop lying, we could be honest about ourselves and see ourselves."

"Never," Marc stood back. His face was composed and his entire being had a look of resolute decision about it. "I'll never do it. If you do, I'll never speak to you again."

I had been quiet as the drama unfolded. I waited now, holding my breath and wondering at the way my plans were working themselves out.

The two of them wouldn't budge. They stood in the center of the room for a while, glaring, challenging. Then Tim turned to me again. "Will you?"

Marc stormed out of the house. I could hear his car engine starting and then the wheels speeding down the driveway.

Reality

We didn't see Marc again for three months.

I hadn't forgotten him — far from it — but it had been long enough that I stopped expecting him to appear.

Summer had ended. An early frost had begun changing the colors of the leaves on the trees. The evenings had a distinct chill to them. But most days were still very pleasant. I was sitting on the front porch of the house enjoying the fading sunlight as the day was ending when Marc drove up. He stopped and got out of the car. He leaned over the roof and seemed to wait for me to say something. I neither welcomed him nor gave any indication that I was displeased that he had shown up.

He came up the stairway onto the porch and sat down beside me. It was obviously a difficult moment and it seemed as though he couldn't look me in the eye. I finally said, "It's been quite a while since you've been by."

"I've been busy," he answered. He was looking down at his hands dangling between his legs.

"College?"

"No. No." He spoke in a low voice, one that carried a tone of defeat more than anything else. But he sighed and seemed to have decided to go on with the conversation, "I never went. I didn't get there."

"What have you been doing?"

"Running."

I took a quick breath. He wouldn't have come to the house unless something was resolved and this was the first indication I had that it might have been what I had hoped.

"Running?" I wanted to give him as much room to move as he needed.

"Yes, running. From you. From Tim. From everything. I nearly got married." He said that suddenly and sat up with a defiant posture, as though he thought I was going to hit him.

"But you didn't."

"No. I couldn't. I was ready to. There was a girl and she wanted to, really badly. It seemed like a good way to handle things. I was blaming all the gay stuff for the confusion I was having. But I kept hearing Tim's voice talking to me about 'honesty' and I couldn't follow through. I couldn't follow through with much — school never happened, I missed the registration deadline 'accidentally but on purpose' — you know what I mean. I kept on having fights at work and I finally quit. I was going to move to Boston, but I never could come up with a decent reason why I should do that, except to get away. It's all been that. Running. Just running."

He wasn't able to go further and I didn't press. "Is he still here? Tim, I mean, is he still with you?"

"Yes." I couldn't help smiling. Not at Marc. I was smiling with the pleasure I'd had over the past three months with Tim. "Yes, he's still here. He's out back, working." I looked at my watch. "It's just about time for him to stop for the day. Come on, we'll go get him and have a drink."

Marc stood up, but seemed to distrust what was going on. I wouldn't comment, but walked through the house. He finally followed me. When we walked out the back door he couldn't help but make a statement. "Jesus! What's been going on? Did Tim do all this?"

"He had some help."

My property had been transformed in those months. The brush had been cleared for tens of feet in all directions. Where there had been wild plants, there was now manicured lawn. Only a few very large, very thick-trunked hardwood trees were left standing. There was one long cleared path from the house all the way to the swimming pond. Along its edge were carefully trimmed bushes.

The lawn that had already existed was still noticeably lush, even after the frost. The weeds were gone and only carefully cut grass remained. I had been very pleased by the result, and I knew it must have looked even more dramatic to someone who hadn't been around for the transition.

I put my hands up to my mouth to form a horn and yelled out Tim's name, then I turned to Marc. "He'll be expecting me to call him about now. He'll come right in. Let's go down by the pond."

We walked along the newly cleared pathway towards the small body of water. It was a man-made improvement on an old beaver pond, about five or six times the size of a large artificial swimming pool. The stream that fed it a constant supply of spring water resumed its own way by spilling over a dam. The water was always clear and clean. It had been one of the main selling points of the house when I had first bought it.

As we were making our way towards the pond, Tim suddenly came into view, walking in the opposite direction. I wasn't worried about his seeing Marc. He must have always known that this encounter was coming and he must have prepared himself for it. Marc didn't say a word. When Tim got up to us, he stopped and looked at me. He didn't say a word. I only told him: "Drinks for two." He nodded and began to move quickly away from us.

Marc turned and watched him go. "God, he's changed that much in only three months! What have you been doing with him?"

"A lot of work; you've seen the grounds."

I took Marc's elbow and turned him back towards the pond. We got to a small collection of lawn furniture near the water and I indicated that he should take a seat beside me.

"He got that muscular in three months?"

"That muscular? Well, yes, he's been cutting down brush, using an axe on trees and a powersaw to make firewood. He's had to lug out the debris. All of that plus the weeding."

"You make sure you can see it, don't you?"

Marc was right. There was little question that Tim's body had developed awfully well in the past months. There had been a good frame and a fine head start when we'd begun; combined with the constant labor of the summer and early fall, the results had been stunning.

And, as he said, I'd made certain that those results could be seen. When he had passed us on his way to the house, Tim had been wearing only the simple racing brief that I allowed for him.

He was carrying the heavy gloves that were a necessity for the rough labor he was doing and he had been wearing his work boots, but that had been the limit of his wardrobe for virtually the whole time he'd been with me.

"Why do you even allow the briefs?" Marc asked. It seemed to be brought on by honest interest. He'd gotten beyond the tension of having come to the house and now there were questions that he wanted answers to only because there were things he hadn't expected.

"A number of reasons. The work is hard and he probably needs to have some support. Also, the suit is made of that stretch fabric that makes his cock and balls look like such an attractive package. I have to admit, though, that a major consideration is simply that it leaves a broad band of white flesh on the midsection of his body. It makes him even more handsome when he's naked." I could have added that Marc would see for himself soon enough, but decided to let that happen naturally.

Just then, Tim came walking down the path with a tray in his hands. When he got to us, he offered each of us one of the two tall drinks he was carrying. I took mine. So did Marc. As soon as he did, he said, "Why haven't you said anything to me?"

Tim smiled, perhaps with a little superior manner, "I can't speak until spoken to, it's part of the training."

"Well, I just spoke," Marc said.

"How are you? I've worried about you."

"You've worried about me?"

But Tim wouldn't respond to the challenge. He put his tray down and, after nodding to me with a small show of obeisance, he walked quickly down to the edge of the pond. There, he took off his boots and socks and then peeled off the tight elastic briefs. The outdoor work had left Tim with a dark tan and it had been so even that it seemed only the small shocking white part of his midsection wasn't brown.

As soon as he was naked, Tim dove into the pond. "It's become very much an evening ritual," I said to Marc. "I look forward to it, watching him bathe." Marc didn't say anything. Tim had a small cache of personal goods that he stored in a nearby waterproof container. He came back to the shore and got soap and shampoo out of it and went about cleaning himself. He would lather up and then dive in again to rinse off. There was one gorgeous moment when he was sudsing up his hair — it was quite long, I'd had him let it grow — and he was standing in just enough depth of the pond that his cock was barely able to float on the surface. His thick pubic hair was plastered against the white skin of his belly and the hard stomach muscles seemed to glide up and out to the expanse of his chest. It was a perfect erotic picture. I could feel my own cock stirring from the image and I knew that Marc had to be responding to it as well.

Then Tim went back to his pack and pulled out a razor. He used the soap to create more lather, but this time only on his crotch and in the crack of his ass. He carefully shaved his balls first, lifting them up in the palm of one hand while the other worked the razor. Then he reached behind himself and pulled apart his ass cheeks and shaved the deep and secret cleft there.

I wanted to explain to Marc how long it had taken Tim to learn how to do it and the reasons I had for insisting that he make this a part of his daily ritual. But the mystery about it that was so rich at this moment was too wonderful to violate with explanations. Whatever reaction Marc was having was more intense than any reasoning I could supply him in any event.

It also must have been very intense for Tim to be doing that now — in front of Marc — without any chance to know what his old roommate and sometime lover was thinking. I only considered it part of Tim's ongoing testing and graded him very well for his ability to continue with his duties in a difficult situation, though I understood that there might even be some pleasure involved for him. Many slaves, early in their education, love to tweak the noses of people who are different than they are.

The late afternoon air was still warm enough that Tim didn't need to towel off after his final swim. He simply shook his head — much as a playful dog might do after a swim — and then walked up the lawn to where we sat. He smiled at both of us, then sat down on the ground near me.

"I guess I can't just ask you how you've been, like I would other people," Marc finally said to Tim.

I put a hand on Tim's damp hair, partly in affection, partly to give him permission to answer.

"Sure you can. I've been fine. I've been happy. I've worked my butt off," he laughed and turned his head so that his face went into the hand I had left there. He nuzzled me, his warm breath on my palm was a delicious counter to the cool wetness of his skin.

"Well, at least you still got your butt," Marc said.

I didn't know if Tim was ignoring the attempt at a joke or if he was playing with Marc, but instead of just answering, he lifted himself up off the ground just enough to look at first the right, and then the left half of his buttocks. "Well, the bruises are gone at least, aren't they," he said very matter-of-factly.

I laughed out loud. Now I knew that Tim was teasing Marc. The blush on the other man's face showed he'd succeeded. He took a sip of his drink and tried to ignore the fun that was being had at his expense.

"I'm sorry," Tim said. He reached across and put a hand on Marc's knee. "I'm really fine. Thank you for wondering, for caring."

"Were there bruises?" Marc's question was serious now.

"Of course there were," I answered. I pulled Tim's head down onto one of my thighs. "There's been a lot to learn and the lessons haven't always been enjoyable. There's been a lot of progress, though, a great deal."

"Progress . . ." The word didn't sit well with Marc. "Tell me about it," he sat up and his voice picked up some power. "Tell me about your progress. How did you achieve it?"

"Sven," Tim answered with a broad smile on his face. "You remember that big major domo that Master was always talking about?"

Master. That was the first time Marc had heard the title applied to me and he physically reacted to the sound with his posture.

"The one on the island?" Marc asked.

"Yes. Master brought him over to help me out." Tim moved his head and pushed it between my legs, an affectionate gesture that left his nostrils breathing warmly on my hardening cock.

"I had listened to all the things that had been said," I explained to Marc. "I knew that Tim wanted to share his experiences with someone and Sven seemed perfect. He was used to that role after all; as the major domo on the island it'd been his responsibility to communicate as much as possible to the new arrivals. The professor was willing to lend him to me."

"What was he really like?" Marc asked Tim.

"You wouldn't have believed him. He was wonderful. He walked onto the property and my knees went weak. I was petrified, for one thing. He looked twice as big as I expected him to be. He was also in love with Master. That didn't make him jealous of me — that I was going to stay here — but it made him damned insistent that everything was going to be done just right or else. And he let me know I was the one who was going to get the 'or else.'

"He worked me like some maniac. Nothing was right. Nothing I did was appropriate. He'd have me crying and feeling like shit . . ."

"Only in the very beginning," I said softly. "Things changed once you got over your fear of him."

"Yeah, they sure did. Marc, it was . . . wonderful. We got to be really close. He taught me lots of things and we'd work together. I've lived in the mountains for a long time, but I didn't know a tenth as much about the forest as he did — that's what he'd studied in college, forestry. We'd get into boots and our briefs and we'd walk for miles while we picked wild flowers for Master. He'd point out all the plants and we found all kinds of streams and ponds I'd never known about.

"Back here, we just learned together, what Master wanted and how. We both knew that we were both trying very, very hard and it helped to understand that. We played, too. You should have seen it when we took our baths together. Sven used to show off a little bit when other people were here. We'd get in the pond and we would always shave each other, that was something that Master had us do to learn to get along. I would have to soap up this giant and shave his chest and legs and even his underarms.

"But when he was in the mood, he'd just take me around the waist, as though I were a little kid, and lift me up with my ass turned this way. Then he'd tell me to spread my ass and, while he was still holding me with one arm, he'd use the razor with the other one."

"Yes," I agreed, "that was amusing."

"*Amusing*," Marc said. He looked away from us. "So you were here playing slavegames with your bodybuilder giant all this time? Working outdoors and having sex. That's all you've been doing."

"That's not the way I'd put it," Tim said. "I've been learning about myself and being happy. And getting excited. I'm working really hard at what I want to do and I'm going to do it."

"What? What is there that you can decide to do here? You're just a plaything for your master."

"I'm going into The Network, Marc. This winter. I'm going to be sold."

"You can't be serious. You can't really mean you're going to follow through with that?"

"But I am serious. I'm very serious. It's been arranged." They stared at one another for a while. Then Tim said, quietly, in the most affectionate voice he'd used so far, "Wouldn't you like to do it with me?"

Marc didn't say a word — perhaps he couldn't. Finally, I pulled Tim back in between my legs. He must have felt my hard cock. He moved against it and I could feel his jaws moving, the hard surfaces producing a pleasurable series of sensations, all of them intensified by his hot breath. Marc only watched. He didn't say anything to either of us.

"He's learned well," I explained, finally. "Once he's had even the slightest indication that a master wants him for any reason, then his own conversations and any distractions have to be dismissed."

Marc and I were staring at one another. I wondered if I'd gone too far with this particular performance and lost him again. But I hadn't, not at all.

"I wanted him to be unhappy. I wanted to come over and see him cringing with fear and being sorry that he ever stayed here that night. I wanted to see something that was even worse than what I had."

"What do you have, Marc?"

"Nothing. I have nothing. I used to have the two of you. But you've ganged up on me. You were my friend and he was my companion. You two were just fine the way you used to be, the way things were. But you had to get together and change everything. You've locked me out."

"No we haven't. You walked out and never even tried to get

back in," I said. " It might have been easier if you had stayed. You could have seen the transitions. This wouldn't seem so . . . extreme if you had watched the stages."

"You mean, if I had been part of them."

Tim had moved. He had been only leaning into me, but now he was kneeling directly in front of me. He wasn't reaching to press against my hard cock any more; instead his face was easily moving around against it and my balls. I could look down and see his own balls and, above them, his hard cock. There was no way anyone could deny his sexual response to what was happening. There was a small sound just then. I had learned to recognize it. It came when he was being so excited that it began to be especially frustrating for him not to touch himself — something that he was strictly forbidden to do without permission. That little sound carried with it a load of erotic pleasure more obvious than almost any other I'd ever heard.

"I don't want to do it," Marc was whispering, I could barely hear him.

"You haven't even been asked to do anything," I said.

"I can't." He spoke as though he hadn't heard what I'd said. "I can't."

"What do you think you do want to do, Marc?"

"Run."

"You told me you'd already done that. Do you really want to start again?" I gently pushed Tim off me. "Go on in, start getting dinner ready. You might as well set another place."

Marc watched his old friend stand up with a stiff erection that had a small dampness around the tip. Tim didn't look at him, but at me. He appeared terribly unhappy, but only about being sent off, not about anything else, at least not at that moment.

When we were alone, I picked up my glass and took another drink. Marc mechanically did the same. "You want me to be like him, don't you?"

"Like him? I'm not sure. Do I want you? Yes. In this kind of sexuality? Yes. But perhaps in a different way. I haven't really thought about that, at least not in any detail."

"You want to sell me into The Network."

"No." I spoke adamantly now. "I don't want to do that. I could. Just as I'm doing it for Tim, because he's asked for it, he wants it. But it wouldn't be what I would want to have happen to you."

"Why not? There's the money . . ."

I waved that away. "I don't earn my income that way and you know it. You've seen how I live. I have more than enough. I would never go out and seduce anyone for it, either. I never have. You've spent enough time at this house in the past few years that you'd know if it had been happening. It wasn't. I have never done that here. I don't recruit for the sake of income.

"I've taken on Tim because it was enjoyable — I won't deny that — I've enjoyed it a great deal. But he asked. You were there when it happened."

"But me?"

"I simply want you."

"To be your slave?"

"I want to live with you. I want to show you a way of life that I think you'd enjoy. I want to teach you things and I want to give you a place to stand and be so you can stop the running, all of the running."

He put an arm on one of his knees and then bent his head down on his palm. I wondered if he was crying. Perhaps he was praying. Whatever was going on, it was a private moment and I decided not to intrude on him. I hadn't been asked to open the door for him — yet.

Fellowship

Marc and I walked back to the house. I took him inside through the front door. I didn't want him to go through the kitchen even though that would have been our route in past times.

We sat in the living room and talked. We avoided the conversations about The Network and Tim. But at least we did talk about more real things than we might have resorted to — or, at least, he might have wanted to escape to.

We discussed his college plans — rather, the lack of them. He confessed that he was becoming concerned with his life again. There might not be many options left. He discussed these topics as though they were irreversible mistakes, things that couldn't in any way be compensated for. That, I knew, wasn't true.

There was a sense in which his problems were caused by the essential frivolity of his lifestyle: The money squandered on new and expensive cars, the constant vacations, the gifts he'd given to each of the succession of boyfriends he'd had over the years and the gifts that others had given him that he hadn't saved.

There were also forces that he had had no control over — being gay, or at least bisexual, in the country, and not having the luxury of living in a community which would have encouraged him to go on to school or rewarded him on those few occasions when he'd done well academically. There had been limited chances in his developing years to even see the possibilities of advancement.

But there was also the truth that there were so many times when he hadn't grabbed hold of an opportunity. There were so many times when someone had made an offer.

The conversation seemed meaningless after a while. He was feeling his regrets earnestly, I didn't doubt that. But the main regret now had nothing to do with academics or career. It had everything to do with the sexual possibilities that were apparent as they flowed between us, no matter what topic we were discussing. Once dinner was served, they'd be even more obvious and they'd have to be dealt with. That was going to be his own problem.

Marc was an alien force in our house, someone different from us. If he thought that the display he'd gotten at the pond was exotic, he was in for something far more that evening.

There's a danger when a stranger enters a fantasy that other people have created. There's the possibility that the beauty that's been produced out of people's imaginations will appear to be ludicrous and inelegant. The laughter of unkind people when they refuse to allow something foreign to them to have its own integrity can sometimes cause great disruption, even pain.

But Tim and I were beyond that. His time with me and the time Sven had spent as a part of the household had created a strong curtain around our existence; the possibility that someone could come in and cause him discomfort was gone — even if it were someone he had known in another life.

"Dinner."

I'd been waiting for the call. I stood up and so did Marc. But he'd been so involved in his own self that he hadn't noticed when Tim had walked into the room. He looked at his old friend now. Tim had a smirk on his face. At another time I would have worked that superior looking expression off him quickly. But he had a right to this moment, I supposed.

"What . . . Where did you get that?"

"Sven," Tim said. He lifted his arms up to give Marc a better view. "He trapped the animals and skinned them himself, right on this property. He designed it here, but it took too long to cure the leather and make the garments by hand, so he had to send it to me."

Tim had been ecstatic about his present and had begged to be allowed to wear it in the house rather than the briefs. The leather loincloth had been colored white; there were two others, one a light brown and the third burgundy. They weren't the barbarian's costumes that Sven himself wore. The Swede had declared Tim too civilized for those. The American needed something that would make him more sensual, not something to give him the appearance of power.

The front was a triangle of leather so wide that it was nearly as full as a pair of briefs, though it didn't extend quite all the way to the sides of Tim's waist. There was hardly any flap, just enough so the inch wide band of leather around his waist could grab hold. There was no back to it, only another band of leather that traveled up the crack of his ass to the same waistband.

Around one of Tim's biceps was a matching band of white leather. On the opposite leg there was a band which was tied at his thigh. Finally, there was a headband, actually necessary since I had wanted his hair to grow out. His carefully trimmed beard and moustache finished the outfit.

Sensual? Yes, it looked very sensual. Sven had done wonders with it all. But the most important thing — and Sven must have known this as well — was that Tim felt sensual when he put on this outfit. It was his sexual uniform. The outdoors work was sweaty; he'd be covered with grime when he finished every day. That bath was no little convenience of mine, it would be necessary. Afterwards, when he came indoors, Tim would leave the elastic briefs outside and he'd go through that special transformation that only clothes can produce, much like the banker who deposits his three-piece suit in a closet and alters his appearance and his self-image when he puts on a pair of jeans and a tight t-shirt before he begins to start his private life.

Marc was stunned. There was no other way to describe it. I wasn't sure why this would have more impact than the image of his friend shaving his ass at the pond, but perhaps the idea of the costume was even more astonishing somehow. And we were inside the house; there was no overlooking the clear purpose of this clothing. He might have been able to ignore the actions at the pond. They were, perhaps, something he could understand or interpret in terms of watching someone wash or shower. He had seen something more intimate than he should have. But he didn't have to think that it had been something that was structured to present an erotic response. These clothes were.

I went into the dining room; Marc followed. A salad was waiting at our place. When we were done, Tim appeared and cleared the plates. Then he brought in the main course on a platter. As I served it, Tim opened and poured wine for us. When he wasn't actually involved in any task, Tim would stand behind me, waiting for a signal for any other request I'd have.

He'd learned to stand with his legs spread apart. His arms were behind his back and his eyes were looking straight forward. Marc would constantly steal glances at him. I knew that Tim wasn't responding. It had been one thing for them to have a conversation at the pond in front of me, but Tim wouldn't have dared to interrupt the meal.

When it was over, I poured out the rest of the bottle of wine and had Marc join me in the dining room. "When does he eat?" That mundane question seemed the most pressing at the moment, at least it was the one that Marc dared to ask.

"Various times," I said. "Sometimes I feed him myself at the table. Now, I assume, he'll quickly eat something while the coffee is brewing."

"Does he always dress like that? Is this a show you're putting on for me?"

"Oh, it's not a show for you, believe that. We didn't know you'd be here, remember. That's his usual clothing, if he wears any."

"Sometimes you don't let him?"

"He's very proud of those outfits that Sven gave him. It can be a subtle, but very effective, means of punishment to deny them to him."

"Was he really bruised?"

"You're still on that? Yes, of course he was."

"Just because you wanted him to be?"

"Marc, we've been through these issues many times. It's no different simply because you know who it is. Just because this isn't one of my stories, doesn't change anything. There are times when I find it beautiful to put him through an ... endurance. There are other times when he needs correction. Either of those — and perhaps still other circumstances — could lead to punishment.

"But I'm tired of this. I want to know about you."

"Me? What about me?"

"What do you want? Really, Marc, what is it that you want? What made you come back here? You didn't have to. You could have just phoned if you were concerned with Tim's well-being. There was no need for you to actually visit."

Tim came in then. He was carrying a tray. He poured and delivered the full cups of coffee to us. Then he sat at my feet. Marc stared at him. "You want me there. I know you want me there."

"I think you might want to be there, Marc." That's all I said. I could see Tim studying his old friend carefully.

"What do you think?" Marc suddenly asked Tim. "Do you think I want to be there?"

"I think you should find out if you like it. You've dreamed it. I know you have. Why don't you find out if this is right?"

"Are you sure it's right for you?" Marc asked.

"I'm more sure now than ever." Tim put his head against my knee. "I want this."

Marc stood up and went to a window. He wasn't looking toward us when he finally spoke. "I can't say I'll do it forever."

"A night," I answered. "Just take it seriously for one night. Join us. See if you can handle it."

"If I can handle it?" he spun around. "I can handle it."

"Then what's your problem?" I asked.

"I'm not sure. I'm frightened of it all."

"You can try it. I would normally never say that one night would be enough. But this is a unique situation. I know it must have been difficult for you to get here. I also know that Tim will be leaving in a few months. You were close once. I'm willing to show you more than you've been able to see so far about what's involved. If you'll enter into this one night understanding that Tim and I mean it to be in earnest."

Then Marc looked at Tim. "Will you help me?" I thought for a moment that Marc would cry. He had made some move he had been struggling against for years.

Tim stood up and went over and put his arms around his friend. "Of course, of course."

I had my glass of wine left. The two of them left to get Marc prepared. I sipped at the burgundy and threw my head back against the chair. I was going to have them both after all! I was going to have them both.

* * *

I was in bed, nude, waiting for them when they were done. Who knows what secrets they told each other? No master ever really knows what goes on in those private conversations. There must be talk about fear and envy, about anticipation and attempts to manipulate situations. Who knows what games they play? Some must have sex of some sort, if only foreplay with one another. Others must argue and fight, getting rid of the discordance that a master would never allow to interfere with his pleasure. Those weren't my concerns at all.

The room was dimly lit. There was still another fireplace here and its flame provided most of the light. I was on the sheets of a king-sized poster bed I'd had constructed on commission. There was plenty of room here for anything that might take place.

But this wasn't really a night for theatrics. This wasn't one of the nights to create a circus. It was to be easy, I had decided. This would be Marc's lesson, his introduction that could lead to other, more intense occasions later on.

Marc seemed strangely shy when they finally walked into the bedroom. They were both naked. "Go to the other side and crawl in," Tim said softly.

They walked to opposite sides of the bed. When Tim was in place Marc put both knees on the surface and moved towards me. "Just follow my lead," Tim was whispering now that they were so close to me and to each other. "Just do what I do or tell you to."

He crawled over to me; Marc did the same. They both put their heads on my belly, just above my crotch. I felt first one, then another hand reach down and fondle my balls. "You have to remember that everything that can cause you pain can cause him pleasure," I could barely hear Tim talking now, his voice was so low. "Handle these carefully, they are something very important."

"Treat them well because he can make ours hurt?"

"Stop it, Marc, just let it happen, don't think everything through right away. Things will come. Just give him pleasure now. It's not something you're used to. None of us are really used to turning ourselves over to creating someone else's pleasure, especially not men. That's why we can be so special, we can overcome it all and do it."

Those were Sven's words. I had heard them when the Swede had been giving Tim his first lessons. I soon could feel the benefits of that education. Tim must have leaned further down first; the mouth that followed must have been Marc's. Both of them were licking my balls soon. Their hands were moving as well. It was as though it were a slightly out of tune duet. One part of one body would do something and then, in a matter of seconds, the other body's same part would mimic the action.

I spread my legs for them as their hands explored underneath me and their fingers probed into the cleft of my ass. Then the mouths moved up along the sides of my inner thighs and my hard cock was trapped between their faces. I could feel the hardness of their noses one minute and then the soft flesh of their cheeks the next.

Two warm, wet tongues now were moving very, very slowly up my stomach. "However fast you want to go, it's too fast," Tim whispered, speaking quickly so his tongue wasn't away from the surface of my body for any longer than necessary.

They moved further. There were two palms that were back on my balls now. Soon, any moment, there would be two hot mouths on my nipples. Tim wouldn't have dared tell Marc why they were taking so long. He could only have hazarded a hope that they were creating an erotic response in me. But there were age-old lessons in what Sven had taught him. They were more delicate and secret than the harsh rules of Tim's biker camp.

No, a slave couldn't always have protection from everything when he had his face between his master's legs. But the slave could please the master and be allowed to stay in the bed. There were always much less desirable activities a master could come up with if the sex play wasn't satisfactory. And there was always the possibility that he could find another favorite. These were time-honored lessons of every sexual slave. Tim knew them.

Then their soft mouths were on my nipples. I reached my hands out. Tim must have given Marc one of the most important lessons. On either side of me I found the matched sets of balls. The legs were spread far apart to make sure nothing could keep me from enjoying the feel of them. As soon as I reached them I found my first pleasant surprise: Marc's were shaven as smoothly as Tim's. That had been one reason their preparations had taken so long. I reached further to see if his anus had been shaven as well; it was. I could feel the tightly gathered skin of his hole and I could sense his shivers as I ran a finger up and down the cleft to create the incomparable sensations that a slave receives when his nude hole is touched.

If this had been any night with any two men, I might have let that play go on for hours. It was utterly enjoyable to have them in my hands and to have their mouths working so erotically on my body. But this night had to be significant. I put my hands on their faces and pulled them off my chest, lifting them up to my own. We all kissed at once. Tim's posture was so much more learned, even after his short training. He had so naturally understood the reasons for so many things that many lessons had come intuitively. His kisses to me were on my cheek, my forehead, small little gestures that carried with them a whole vocabulary of submission.

Marc's were much less studied, and much more passionate. We kissed each other on the mouth. While Tim was moving around so quickly. Marc and I were exploring each other more intimately, perhaps as lovers would. But that was one possibility, that this was our chance to fall in love and we both understood it.

Then I pushed them aside. Marc was immediately disoriented. His cock had leaked pre-come on my cover. I didn't care, but he seemed embarrassed as he looked at it. Then he made a movement that he instantly knew was ridiculous; he tried to cover his hard-on, the source of the dampness and the proof of his excitement. I gestured to Tim and he slid off the side of the bed onto his feet.

I moved to get off the mattress. Tim quickly made way for me and was standing on the floor beside the bed. I waved to Marc to follow. By the time he'd gotten to the space between the fire and the bed where I'd gone, I was already opening the doors of a cabinet there. Tim stiffened when he saw me doing this. At another time, it would have meant that he had failed to arouse me in the more gentle arena and it was his own fault that I was turning to this alternative.

Marc, of course, couldn't have known any of those intricacies. I found what I wanted and turned to Tim. "Show yourself."

He went into position at once. "This," I said for Marc's benefit, "is the way a slave displays himself to his master. His arms are behind his neck, leaving his chest and underarms open, exposed, vulnerable. His legs are spread far apart, he wants his cock, balls and anus to be easily accessible to the master. His head faces straight forward. He has no need to watch what's being done to him because he knows he will accept it in any event."

I moved towards Tim and reached up to his chest. I had a pair of clamps in my hand. I attached one to each of his nipples. They were extremely harsh, so painful I had usually kept them only for special punishment duty. But this would be a good lesson for Marc. Tim's face grimaced when each of the two metal contraptions were attached. I quickly applied a small band of leather around the base of his balls after that. It was tight enough that it forced his testicles to strain against the very bottom of his sac.

"Look at him now. See how he's kept his position and how the slightest pieces of chain and leather make him so much more attractive." I ran a hand across Tim's belly. He was already sweating from the exertion. There was a strong odor coming from under his arms and his stomach was damp with perspiration.

"Look how much better he looks than you do." I swiveled to face Marc. "You're standing there awkwardly, your arms dangling at your sides, you don't know where to put your hands, your hard-on is embarrassing you. Why don't you copy him? Come on, Marc. Display yourself."

His movements were much slower than Tim's instant compliance, but he did it. He stared at me — not into the distance as he should have — but I appreciated the fear and excitement on his face so very much I didn't reprimand him.

When he was in position, with his fine arms over his head and so nicely stretched to show off his own muscles, I complimented him, "Don't you feel better now? More graceful? You are. You look much more handsome that way with all of your best features open for view. It's such a shame that men are always hiding those very things that would make them so appealing to others — their cocks, balls, the recess of their asses. And even their legs are so often covered that we can't appreciate them nearly as much as they deserve to be."

I walked up to him and ran the same hand over his body. His cock was still stiff and erect. I let my hand fall to his genitals and hold his newly shaven balls once more. Then I reached up and my finger traced the line of a thick blue vein from the base of his cock all the way down the shaft until it disappeared into the thick purple skin of the cockhead.

"Are you really ready?"

He nodded, his brow a mass of wrinkles. He seemed amazed he was here and allowing this to happen. It might have been too much to demand that he say yes out loud. I had another pair of tit clamps in my free hand. I applied them to his erect nipples. They were much less severe than Tim's had. But, after all, he hadn't had Tim's training. The very idea of being in front of two other men and seeing his naked body adorned in that fashion was more than enough of a trial for him — at least for now. He sucked in his breath as each of the rubber-tipped machines bit into him. I also wrapped a band of leather around his balls.

Then I stood back. In the firelight they were extraordinarily handsome. Actual rivulets of sweat were running down Tim's sides now. Those clamps were very harsh and the physical response was all I had hoped from him. I loved watching him in all of his tests of endurance. When Sven had been here and he had entered into a full-blown case of hero-worship of the big Swede, Tim had vowed to never say no and to never plea for escape. Sven hadn't; he wouldn't. Now, the fact that Marc was here and witnessing him reproduced the same pride in him.

"I never asked," I finally began, "when you two were together, who fucked whom?"

They were both taken back by the question. Marc finally answered, "Tim usually did it to me, but not always."

"Then we should have a new start, don't you think?"

Neither one of them spoke; they didn't dare. I moved back to the cabinet and pulled out a few more things. I moved over to Marc and, after I put down a bottle of lubricant on a nearby surface where I'd be able to reach it easily, I opened the condom wrapper that I had retrieved. I started to talk to Tim. "This will be good, don't you think? To show him how well you've learned to be fucked? You didn't do it very handsomely when you first came here, not at all. But Sven helped, didn't he?"

"Yes . . . , sir."

"Tell him."

I started to unravel the condom over the length of Marc's cock while Tim's voice struggled to tell the story. "Sven would be beside me while I was getting fucked by Master. He would talk to me, whisper in my ear all the secrets of how to do it the right way. I'd follow all of his instructions."

"Just the way you did when he told you how to suck cock?"

"Yes, sir."

"And other things he told you?"

"All the other things he told me. He would be beside me while Master did . . . whatever he wanted and he would show me how to give Master the most pleasure possible while they were happening."

The condom was covering Marc's erection now. "You get to see the benefits of all that education. Follow me, keep your hands up high and your legs spread. I'll do the work for you."

I led the one naked man over to a position where he was standing behind the first. I put my hand on Tim's neck and guided it downwards. "Look how beautiful a slave can be. His legs are so far apart and now he's leaning over at his waist. There's nothing that could possibly interfere with anyone who wanted to have a good fuck from him."

I ran a hand over Tim's ass and could feel the way the skin was stretched tautly by the unusual but graceful position. "He is more muscular now, isn't he? He must have gained at least fifteen pounds in these few months, all of it hard and well-proportioned."

I took hold of Marc's sheathed cock and pulled him the few inches forward until the tip made contact with the bunched brown skin of Tim's anus. Then I reached and got the lubricant. I poured some of the grease over the condom and then used the residue to slip into the tight, hot pocket of Tim's ass.

"You'll be amazed by how well he's learned this," I said to Marc. Then I pushed him forward until his cock slipped directly into the asshole. Marc let out a sharp sigh as his cock was gripped by the heated muscles. "He's taking hold of you," I explained. "He's been taught not to fight you, but to let you in and then to clamp down to make sure you have the most intense sensation. Now, pull back, just a little." Marc did as I told him to.

"Stand still. He's been trained to do the fucking if you want, haven't you, Tim?"

"Yes, sir." His voice was strained from the sex and the tension of leaning over. But he began to move back and forth, letting his anus hold on to Marc's cock just at the head and then pushing backward to have the whole length of it slide in until Marc's pubic hair was pushing against the shaven area right around his hole.

"Slowly, Tim, slowly, let Marc understand what it must be like."

Tim groaned, I wasn't sure if it was frustration or agony. But he made his motions even more languid. I looked at Marc. "Don't change a thing," I said. "Don't grab hold of him or try to make it go faster. Don't do anything but enjoy what's happening. Then try to think of yourself on the other end. Think what it would be like to be bending over on command and having some other man's condom-covered cock up your ass. But don't think of it in terms of pain or humiliation, think of how you could make it better for him."

I moved around until I was standing in front of Tim. His hips were still moving back and forth with exquisite slowness. I took another condom and rolled it out onto my erection. Without needing to be told, Tim opened his mouth. "He's trained not to do anything but be ready," I explained to Marc. "It's not his place to decide to suck it; it's only his purpose to prepare himself in case I want him to."

Then I lunged forward and the length of my cock went down Tim's willing mouth. "This is his reward," I said as I allowed Tim's motions move his head up and down my cock as his hips moved back and forth to take Marc's shaft. "He's waited for this since the moment he saw you walking onto the lawn."

I felt my orgasm approaching, but I didn't want it so soon. I pulled my latex-covered cock out of Tim's mouth. He moaned again. A part of it must have been simply from the exertion, but it was just as much the hurt of having my body taken away from him.

I moved over to Marc and gently put my hands on his waist. I pulled him back until he understood that I wanted him to stop fucking. He looked at me with a confused and regretful expression, but complied.

"Get back in position, both of you." They did. Now with the activity stopped, Tim was left only with the tight and torturous bite of the clamps on his nipples. He looked down at them, helpless and clearly in pain. I reached over and lifted up the chain that connected the two metal devices. The simple act of removing even a slight amount of the tension created a wave of agony so great that his knees actually seemed to buckle slightly and the groan that roared out of his chest was certainly honest.

His hands involuntarily jerked off the back of his neck and would have moved to stop me if he hadn't stopped himself quickly. He was embarrassed, ashamed that he'd cracked even slightly. The arms were securely positioned again without my having to have to say anything. We stared at one another. I watched his resolve take a firm hold once more.

I put a hand on his cheek and he reached down to run his tongue over the surface of my palm. He closed his eyes. His own imagination was transforming the actions back into the romance that he so fervently wanted.

I turned to Marc. For the first time he seemed to want to offer something. It seemed that he lifted up his chest. He expected me to play with his nipples as well and he was telling me that he was prepared.

I went behind him and ran a hand over the firm ass. Unlike Tim, whose body hair included a cover over his buttocks, Marc's rear was smooth, almost silky to my touch. He tried too hard. Thinking my touch was a command, he bent over as though he assumed he was the next one to get fucked.

"No, no," I said softly, drawing him back up to a standing position. "I want to show you more of what Tim's learned."

I kissed him on the side of his face and raked my fingers through his hair. Then I returned to Tim.

There were tears forming at the corners of his eyes. The sensations on his nipples must have come close to unbearable by now. "Please," he whispered.

"Do you think this is all that might happen to you in The Network?" I mocked. "You want to be sold, to live in that world, and you're concerned about a little pressure on your tits? Perhaps you're not as ready as I had thought."

"I am." He drew upon whatever strength he still had.

"You just want me to make it easier and shackle you, so you don't have to use your own resources to maintain your posture. That's so easy for all of you, to have bondage remove your options, to have your hands and feet tied so you can believe things are being done to you without your complicity."

He blushed. He wouldn't have known this shame three months ago, but he did now. The lessons had taken hold wonderfully. This particular one was done. There was no need to continue with it. I took hold of each of the two clamps and removed them at once.

Tim couldn't restrain himself now. He doubled over with the sudden rush of blood into the restricted flesh. He cried out in pain. I listened while he struggled to regain control of his breathing. As soon as he had, he began to straighen out, but, in the middle of the motion, he kissed the side of my neck — a small and beautiful gesture to ask my forgiveness.

"Go to Marc, show him your abilities with your tongue."

I didn't have to be explicit. He knew I was encouraging some creativity now. He moved over to where the other man still stood with only the easier clamps and the leather strap on his body. Tim knelt with a fine grace. He moved to the floor in one fluid gesture. As he'd been taught, he left his legs wide apart. He bent over even further and I could see his lips touch the top of Marc's feet.

Then the small pink tongue came out and began to wash the surface of the skin. Slowly, he moved up Marc's legs. He came to the two testicles that were drawn up tightly against Marc's underbelly after minutes of careful progress. Then he lifted first one, then the other up with his tongue, washing each of them with long laps that left a covering of his spit on the sac.

Marc was responding to the attention. His cock was rampant again. Small drops of liquid oozed from the slit. I put a finger there and gathered some up, feeling the viscous stuff.

"You could be down there," I said quietly. "If you stay, you'll be down there for a long, long time, just as he has been." I played with Marc's nipples then, teasing the clamps with slightly more pressure, lifting their chain, tugging at them slightly. It was all I did, just that. It was all Marc was feeling along with Tim's tongue on his balls. But it was enough.

Marc shot pulsing waves of come out of his cock and onto Tim's hair. The white ooze sank into my kneeling slave's long locks and darkened them where it had landed.

I stood back and looked directly into Marc's eyes. "You weren't given permission to do that."

I will always treasure the memory of Marc's face. It was swept up into an orgy of fear and anticipation. It was the most handsome moment of his life.

An Idea Takes Hold

I was vaguely aware of Tim's movements the next morning as he slipped out from under the covers. He left the room to go downstairs to begin his day. But this time I wasn't left alone. There was still Marc.

I reached over and wrapped one arm over the top of the young man. He initially tried to push me away. He must have still been deep in sleep. But he seemed to suddenly remember where he was and what had happened last night. His stiffened body relaxed suddenly, letting my arm pull him close to me.

I slipped my other arm underneath him to make my hold on him even more secure. He didn't resist. In fact, he moved closer to me. I was facing his back and now I could feel the whole of its broad expanse against my front. His hard round buttocks pushed against my crotch and let my erection nest in the cleft of his ass.

My fingers moved and found his nipples. They were raw from the night before. I only had to graze them to get a quick response. But, as he'd proven last night, Marc was not going to quit. He melted back into my arms, refusing to let the physical discomfort of his nipples keep him from my body.

I only had to remember the red stripes that would still be there on his ass to have my cock go from enjoying itself to needing release. I let it slip and slide up and down the crack of Marc's ass. The smooth, shaved skin was satin-soft. I could feel the natural hairlessness of Marc's chest and the results of last night's play on his scabbed nipples and I was driven on towards orgasm.

Driven. That's the only word I could possibly use. I rolled my hips back and forth to use my cock's foreskin to let me glide over his ass and then, in a short time, I shot a load of come onto the crevice. I sank onto my back, slowly extricating my arms from his body.

He turned over on to his side to face me. He had a hurt look on his face. Before he could say anything, Tim appeared in the doorway with a single cup of coffee in his hand. He put it on the stand by the bed.

He was still naked. His cock was hard as well. I could see the puffed flesh of his chest where those clamps had so viciously bitten him last night. I could also see the stripes on his hips and thighs where the lash had attacked.

I smiled as I thought all that: . . . *those clamps had so viciously bitten him, . . . the lash had attacked.* No, no, they hadn't. Those were inadequate descriptions. I had done it. *I had made love to him last night?* No, that didn't work well either. The language was simply too limited to be able to express the reality.

I stopped worrying and took the cup. While I sipped it, I used my other hand to draw Marc in close to me. I directed his head to the closer of my own nipples and he obediently began to suck. Tim was looking down at the scene, his cock still erect. He obviously wanted something to help him relieve that pressure. Marc too evidently wanted something: His cock was stiff now as it pressed against my thigh.

I pushed Marc away and took more of the coffee. "You'll learn to live with that." He didn't understand, I could see it in his eyes. "The burden of the slave is his erection; the thing which makes his master all the more awesome is the control he has over it. You'll learn that your sexual pleasure is the least of my concerns, other than in its usefulness as a means of rewarding — or punishing — you."

I sat up and my movements pushed the covers down further. Marc looked down at his hard cock as though it was something foreign now. He was studying it, but also understanding that he could do nothing to it — if he wanted to stay. But that hadn't been decided.

I gestured for Tim to get back into the bed with us. He approached cautiously. He knew after last night that Marc's presence didn't mean that there would be any lessening of discipline in the house. In fact, he had good reason to suspect that I was enforcing it even more as an example to his old roommate.

But he did climb on top of the sheets and moved quickly up against me. I sat there with both of them and their hard cocks pressing on my flesh. This was my moment, more, in its own way, than last night had been.

I finished the coffee and put the empty cup down. I ruffled both their heads, messing their hair and embracing them even more. We laid there silently for a moment while I luxuriated in the feel of it all.

"What will we do today?" I finally asked. Marc didn't speak or move. Tim nuzzled closer, his face burrowed in the space between my arm and chest.

"What do you usually do now?" Marc asked.

"Tim would make breakfast. Then, perhaps, we'd play a bit, try out a new toy, maybe I'd want to have sex again." Tim's body reacted to the simple statement. . . . *try out a new toy* had nothing to do with innocent recreation. I was sure Marc understood that.

"Then, there'd be work to do. The house, the yard, whatever, while I went about the business I needed to attend to. Lunch would follow. A nap — usually together." Tim actually relaxed when I spoke now. Those naps were always among the most gentle times for him. When, for whatever reason, they hadn't been shared between us, they were something that he and Sven could have together.

"There might be shopping in the afternoon, or more work. There'd be dinner to prepare, then eat. Finally reading, perhaps a movie on the video machine. In there, as often as not, there'd be another opportunity to have sex, of some kind."

" 'Of some kind,' " Marc said, lifting his head up and looking back and forth between Tim and myself. I think that was the first moment that he had actually noticed the marks on Tim's buttocks. He reached over and ran his fingers over the skin.

"What do you think of them?" I asked.

He pursed his lips and then reached across my body and put a series of small kisses on the red welts. He placed the side of his head on one of Tim's firm asscheeks. "I don't know how you can do it. Just this way."

The three of us were now all touching one another. I had the warm weight of Marc leaning over the middle of my body, his cock was caught pressing against my side. Tim was facing me. "I think that's a very silly question given the circumstances. This is possibly the most enjoyable way to do it I can imagine."

"But it's so ordinary," Marc whispered. "It's not theatrical, it's not anything unusual."

"What do you mean?"

"If . . . If we were in the city, at one of the leather bars that Tim and I used to go to, and you were in leather . . . If it was a trip, a night, a trick . . . That I can understand. But this is so complete. There's no relief from this.

"Last night. . ." He faltered even more now than he did when he had been struggling to get the words out just before, and there was an excruciating moment while he tried to get his speech back. "Last night was all those things that you read about. There was the excitement and the sense that it could happen because it was going to end. I was going to wake up this morning and I'd just be able to put on my clothes and leave.

"Maybe we'd have something to eat together. And, like the other times, we wouldn't talk about anything, we'd make believe it didn't really happen the night before, not that way."

" 'Like the other times?' " I asked the question, but Tim had lifted his head up sharply when he heard that.

"I told you I've been running. But not always in one direction. I've been to New York, trying to see what this was all about, what it was that Tim would leave everything so as to have it. And what it was that it would make me so crazy, having dreams about it.

"I did it the other way — with handsome men in uniforms and leather costumes. They weren't like this. It was never the same waking up the way it was this morning, with you just taking it all up again and Tim never leaving the role. It was always different. I could handle it so much more easily.

"It was as though I was an actor in a play. No one really expected me to continue the role when the curtain came down. Sometimes that meant that I had to follow through or play along until I left the physical apartment. There were some people — couples, mostly — where they'd be a little bit like you and Tim in the morning. But I would already know that it was either a scene being strung out for my benefit or else just a longer trick than usual. Some men would do it for a night, some for a weekend. That all made sense to me."

"Why?" I asked.

"Because it made the sex better, more. It made everything so intense." He moved up, off of Tim, and laid his body onto mine. His arms went around my shoulders and his head rested on my chest now. "But I was only having sex with their roles. Never them. You want me to do it with you and then wake up and discover that going to work, making a meal, even watching television is a continuation of it.

"I don't think I can do this."

Tim reached up and put his arm around Marc's middle. I could see him squeeze slightly to give his old friend a fraternal show of confidence. Marc looked over at him. Then he remembered something. He turned to me."Can I ask him some questions?"

I nodded, almost amused that he was taking rules so seriously in the middle of his unsure place.

"Why do you want to go to The Network instead of staying here? What's the difference?"

Tim thought for a moment, "I want the adventure of it. I don't have any better answer than that. I might end up in a household just like this one, I know that. I might end up doing nothing more than I do now. But it will be with a different person and I know it will mean I'll learn something different just for that reason. It'll mean I'll have taken a greater risk. And it means that I can't retreat into the familiarity of this place.

"There's always the fact that this is near my home. This is the place I grew up. I want to stretch something in my life."

"You see, that's one of the problems. It was so hard to come here yesterday because this is all so familiar. It's where I live too. Last night, with the fireplace going and the strange light and the careful way you two did everything, I could suspend everything and make believe I was in one of those tricks' 'dungeons' in New York. But now it's morning and out there is the pond where I used to go swimming every day. I don't know if I can just change everything so much that I can forget that."

"You want a curtain?" I asked Marc seriously. "You want a way to make a transition?" He nodded. "But you've been doing this exploration in the cities. Wasn't that enough?"

"No. It was with strangers and they aren't the same as you two. Even now, I'm going to have to go through watching Tim again this morning doing all those things in those ways. It's more . . . it's more everything — dangerous, frightening, strange . . ."

"Do you want a curtain to help you with the two of us or do you want it so you don't have to face it — really face it?"

"'It?'" he asked. "I'm not even sure what 'it' is when you talk that way."

"Tim's going to leave. You and I will stay here. You could stay with me alone. There are so many ways that you make it sound as though you want to. I want it as well. We could, if you're willing, construct our own contract. I could put you through college. You want it; I can provide it."

"And I could become like Sven?" His voice was so distant sounding that I couldn't decipher the cause. Was he picturing a dream or was he having flashes of a nightmare?

"Sven didn't know what he was going to do when he started, at least he claims he didn't. Tim doesn't know what he'll choose to do after his contract with The Network is done, either. I don't need to know what your next decision will be when we might be done."

"Oh, that's not true." Marc burrowed his face into my flesh again, then rested it on my shoulder. "You want me to stay here for a long, long time. You'll do everything you can to keep me here. Tim is a project. You're like me, actually. The theatrics are easy for you and you enjoy your little trips with your friends in The Network a lot. You've had a great time with Tim here, doing the training and all the structuring and having the bodybuilder come. But you want something different from me, I can tell that.

"Not just that you want me to stay. But you're going to want . . . more. What is that?"

I didn't want to talk about these things now. Nor did I want to lose Marc. I'd waited too long to reenter this world and I'd overlooked his potential for too many years. But there was a way.

"I'll give you a chance to have your ritual, your curtain. We'll give you a transition. It can be quite easy. I'd already thought about going away soon. You haven't any commitments, you've said that clearly enough. You've lost your job and you never registered for school. Then you can't have any reason to stay here.

"We'll go somewhere else. Not to the cities you've already been to where the way you did things was to 'trick,' as you put it. I loathe that word, the way it demeans the sexual exchanges that men have with one another. I don't want to simply transpose us on to that. But we'll go away. You can try it on with an audience — that will scare you, but at least the audience will be made up of strangers and you can deal with the eyes looking at you without needing to face ones you already know — at least this time."

"A trial?" Marc asked.

"Not in any usual sense," I responded. "A 'transition,' that's a much better way to put it, I think. A way to begin."

"But I told you that I don't think I can do this," he complained. "I really don't know..."

"I know that if we stay here and think about it, you'll never be able to. But if we go to a different place, then you can see your strengths and you can test your desires. It's the best way."

He didn't argue anymore. He and Tim were quiet now, their hard cocks were both leaking onto my skin and both of them — not possibly knowing that each was doing it — began to rock their bodies against mine. The idea had taken hold.

Moving into the Arena

Any comparison between the art of modern sexual slavery and the institutions of slavery in history is dangerous. Those ancient forms carry with them implications that do damage to the facile creativity engaged in by the people of the sexual underground.

But there are moments when a parallel asserts itself and can inform and entertain us. One of those occurred to me as the three of us were walking down a crowded street in the Southern beach resort two days later.

I imagined a vanquished barbarian giving his allegiance to a Greek conqueror in ancient times. It probably had been something very difficult for him to do; it may well be beyond our ability to comprehend the humiliation he suffered. His life had been spared on the battlefield. He must have thought that he was the one who was to blame for the fact that he lived. He hadn't fought hard enough to join his comrades in whatever heaven they believed in.

So, he had no choice but to give himself to his new lord as a slave. There was bitter defeat in the act of bowing to his new master. But it was his fate. There, on his knees before an arrogant Greek, he might even have thought that this was his due. His tribe had been bested by other warriors. It must be that their gods wanted this new power to rise over them.

There could have been a certain nobility in all that. His master was the better on the battlefield. And, to the ancients, that meant he was a better man. The chains that the newly enslaved barbarian wore were made — in his mind — of the same metal as his lord's sword. *So be it*, he might have thought.

I had not conquered Tim and Marc. I had simply allowed them to enter a certain world. But in our mountain retreat they had seen only the slavery that existed between myself and them. They had only seen their Greek lord in his armor.

But the barbarian slave, after his moments of grace in defeat, would eventually have to be taken to market. He would have to walk through the crowds of housewives and peasants who would gawk at him and make jokes. No longer only submitting before a military hero, he would find that he was possibly going to be sold to a lowly merchant and would find his slavery not the payment of his debt to his physical better, but a cruel twist of fate that made him into a shackled clerk.

I envisioned that as Marc and Tim's predicament as we made our way through the crowds. This was the bazaar where the warriors were displayed to the soft and unworthy civilians. My two slaves in their finery, with their handsome uniforms, were only two more males who were available to anyone who wanted to look at them.

Marc had wanted this transition and I was giving it to him. I only hoped he'd see how tawdry this alternative was and, instead, learn to love the intensity that could be created with a certain elegance in our mountain retreat.

I had decided to underscore the dramatics of it all to the two young men as soon as we had arrived. After we had checked into our guest house, I had taken them immediately to one of the leather stores that line the main street. Here the office workers from cold northern cities and the timid souls from midwest towns who would never dream of entering the world of sexual creativity went on a vacation binge and bought themselves outfits that they would never have worn at home.

It had been perfect for my purposes. Instead of the exquisite loincloths that Sven had made for him, I had Tim dressed in a factory-made costume. The same for Marc who, as a result of his own request, was now wearing the uniform of the urban male on the quest for the perfect trick. That phrase was a contradiction in terms. But that would never be understood by someone who didn't realize that spontaneous moments can never equal the results of years of learning and the accretion of years of another man's mastery.

They had on typical black leather boots, the ones that people suppose bikers wear. I imagined that Tim was able to remember back and realize that not one of his old friends would ever have had anything on his feet that had the polish his had at this moment. They also had shiny black leather chaps to cover their old blue jeans. The chaps did have a purpose: They outlined the crotches in front and the asses in back, forcing the eye to recognize the superb bunches of flesh in both places.

Of course, when I saw those gathered and displayed sections of a male's body, I understood the possibilities they held in a different way than most other people. I could see the men who watched my handsome young charges walk down the street. Those faces had all the marks of desperate desire — but desire to suck the fat cocks that Marc and Tim displayed or to touch the firm asses. The more . . . subtle options of the lash and tight rawhide bindings weren't so obvious to others.

I led them into one of the many gay bars. It had advertised itself as "leather." As soon as we walked in, the early afternoon crowd paid immediate attention. Before they even were aware of the young men's attractiveness, they saw their t-shirts. I had bought them at the same store as their chaps. The shirts were black. In bold print across their chests was white block lettering that spelled out: SLAVE.

The ancient barbarian would have had to carry some public identification of his status — his chains or his collar would have made his humiliating slavery obvious in the crowded bazaar. Why should these two have any less obvious display of their status?

If they noticed the stares, Marc and Tim didn't give any indication of it. I sent Marc off to buy us cold drinks. As he went I was certainly aware that both of them were humbled. But not just by this situation. The time in the shop had scared them so much more that they hadn't overcome it yet.

There had been the two clerks, first of all. They'd been large, muscular men who gave off an extremely strong odor — the mixture of their own perspiration and the smell of the leather that had been sticking to their flesh for the whole warm and humid day. They'd eyed Marc and Tim openly, sizing up their bodies and their sexual potential.

As soon as I began to give the orders and make the judgments, the two brawny clerks caught on to what was happening and spent the rest of the time they waited on us rubbing in the degradation I encouraged. They'd felt up the two younger men's bodies, openly grabbing their cocks and balls and slapping their asses. They would make the most debasing comments when clothes were tried on — insisting at one point that they should buy the smallest available t-shirts since they claimed the normal size wouldn't let anyone get a good look at the sharp points of the slaves' tits. Those two men knew perfectly well how those nipples had been developed.

Marc and Tim had been so shaken by the rough manner of the two other men that I wondered just how I was going to arrange a situation where they would have to submit to even more from them. The lessons were certainly valuable for both. They weren't used to seeing just how vulnerable their status made them. To suddenly have older, stronger men standing by their booths while they changed clothing had really gotten to them. They had gotten over their inhibitions about my studying them, and they had learned to expect me to comment on even the most intimate details of their bodies and clothing. But to have a stranger make an evaluation of the curves of their asses or the adequacy of their cock size was a sudden shock to both.

When Marc had brought back our drinks, the three of us stood against a wall and surveyed the crowd. "If I were to give you away, which one here would you want to have fuck you?" I asked Marc.

He was startled at first. "Give me away?"

"I certainly will have that right, you know."

He looked around the group and finally pointed to one man about his own age who was obviously looking back. "Him."

"Why?"

"Because. . ." he had no good reason.

"You're only picking out the one who's the most attractive in the most usual sense," I said. "You shouldn't settle for that." I made my own quick evaluation. "Him, over there in the corner, the one with the jeans with the holes in them, that's the one you should have chosen."

"Yes," Tim agreed.

I was amused by that. "And just why?"

"Look at his balls, they're hanging far down his left thigh. And the keys, there's a bunch of them hanging on his left. He has a belly — there's no denying that. But those balls have been through things, you can tell. And the keys may not mean he'll be like you, but at least he knows what he wants and what he wants is just the thing that I'd probably want to give him."

"Good answer." The man had the appearance of someone who had, in fact, been around a good deal. His face was older than mine, and his hair wasn't very well taken care of. But there was also bulk in his arms; the stomach that protruded over his belt line would be solid and firm. There was also a look about him. It was one that said he was hungry, so hungry that I was quite sure I would have had the best luck with him, not either one of my keeps. But I wouldn't destroy their illusion so quickly. They would learn soon enough that it was difficult to find someone who was naturally inclined to be on top.

Various men would come up to us and talk. I'd banter with them, but Marc and Tim were under strict discipline. They knew better than to speak without my permission. Eventually, each of the visitors would pick up the intensity of what was passing between us and would retreat, almost as if burned by us. There would be an occasional rude comment about us, or about me. That always was a simple display of jealousy and I reacted to it as such.

I was ready to go back to the guest house when the two men from the leather shop came in. I nodded to them and smiled. They came over and joined us after stopping at the bar. They had extra drinks for us in their hands. "This is what Mike told us you were drinking," one of them said as he handed the glasses around.

"Thank you." I was the only one who spoke. That brought a smirk from the first clerk, the one who had carried the drinks.

"I'm Sam; this is Joseph," he said. I shook their hands. They had picked up enough to realize that they shouldn't exchange the greeting with the other two. Marc and Tim simply became more uncomfortable and shifted nervously on their feet.

We passed small talk that gave Sam and Joseph enough time to continue the minute examination of the two SLAVE-shirted males beside me. Joseph seemed to understand the most. While we talked he would run a hand across one or another of the two in a casual manner, simply testing their flesh.

I liked the two of them. They turned out to own the store together. They had another one in a different resort where the season was complementary to here. They made their lives traveling between one of the tourist spots and the other.

They were older than Marc and Tim. I guessed them to be more than thirty. They were taller as well, each of them at least my own six feet. Sam had balding hair which looked attractive on him, especially with the thick black moustache over his mouth. He was wearing a worn leather vest over an athletic t-shirt. There was a piece of rawhide gathered on his left side and tied to one of his belt loops. Another was tied across his firm left bicep. His jeans were even more worn than the vest. While there was no rip, yet, the crotch was worn nearly white and the seat of his pants showed bare threads.

Joseph was blond. He, too, wore a moustache. His skin was a dark tan from the constant sun his seasonal travels allowed him to indulge in. His muscles were even more developed than Sam's; Joseph had put more time into his body and had been rewarded with larger results. His clothing was essentially the same as Sam's, though the jeans were less worn and the vest newer. The shirt was tight enough that I could make out small rings decorating his pierced tits. He also had the length of rawhide on his right bicep. Since the arm was bigger, the effect was even more impressive. I felt myself respond to him.

I enjoyed talking to the two new people. I enjoyed the effect they had on Marc and Tim even more. They had reacted so strongly to Sam and Joseph in the store that they had probably been relieved when I had brought them to the bar. To find their tormentors standing here, as well, created major anxiety. They moved from foot to foot and their eyes darted crazily as they tried to gauge if there was any danger here — was I going to create a scene that they'd have to endure?

I decided to play on it. I told Marc and Tim to go back to the guest house. I would meet them there later. I wanted to go to lunch at another bar and invited Sam and Joseph to come with me as my guests.

The two young men who moved quickly to follow my directions were very nervous, so nervous that deep and loud masculine laughs from the leather storekeepers followed them out the door.

* * *

They were waiting in the room when I returned after my meal. They were naked, as they had been told to be once they were inside the closed door. They looked at me with apparent dread. They were still concerned with Sam and Joseph and what we might have planned. At least now they had reason to be.

"I want to show you off at the pool. Put on your briefs." They jumped up and got their swimming suits. They had pulled them on and were waiting for me while I was still undressing. I pulled on my own suit and then turned to look at them. "No, that's not enough of a display."

Neither one spoke. Marc put his arms around his chest; even though it was very hot in the nearly tropical climate, he looked as though he was shivering. I went to my suitcase and pulled out two rawhide strings. I sat on the edge of the bed and waved them over to me.

When they were standing in front of me, I pulled down both their briefs. They both were getting the start of an erection in response to the rude nudity of having their swimming suits caught on their knees.

I took one of the pieces of rawhide and weaved an extravagant web around Marc's cock and balls. It not only separated each testicle from the other, it wrapped around to create another separation between the cock and balls. The package trapped the blood that had flowed to his cock, leaving him with a partial hard-on that wasn't going to go away for a long time.

I repeated my handiwork on Tim. When I was done, I insisted on pulling up their briefs myself, not even allowing them the self-sufficiency of doing it themselves. The result was a much larger and more prominent bulge in the cup of the suits. Both their cocks were forced up and to a side, the half-engorged heads were easily seen through the stretch fabric. Anyone whose eye was at all trained would also be able to see the evidence of the rawhide around the clearly discernible balls as well.

Now, I told them, we were ready for their public. That phrase hung in the air as we went downstairs and found a place on the patio around the guest house pool. I took a long chaise longue and Tim and Marc found inflatable cushions they could bring over and spread on the stone surface nearby.

When I had Tim go and get drinks from the poolside bar, he used the errand as an excuse to pose a question. "What did you mean, 'ready for our public?'"

"Well, since you are going to give a performance tomorrow evening, I thought it was only right that you should get used to the idea of being on more intimate display than you have been."

"Please," Tim was being very careful to word this correctly, "what do you mean when you say we're going to give a performance?"

"There's a very special AIDS benefit tomorrow evening at the leather bar. Sam and Joseph told me about it. It seems that what they call the leather community here has come up with a particular form of public service that will raise money."

"What is it?" Tim couldn't stand it when I stopped talking and had to ask more.

"A slave auction." I let that sink in while I sipped my drink. "It seems that the men of the community offered themselves up for bids. The money goes to the charity and the high bidder is able to indulge in the services of the purchased man for the evening. It is an admirable thing — to raise money for the cause. It's also wonderful training. You will be going on the real block soon enough and I thought you might as well get a sense of what it will be like and how you will react to it. Marc may never see those auction blocks. But he should be able to understand more what will be going on if he's had at least this experience.

"Of course, you'll both need more of a . . . costume to carry it off. But Sam and Joseph have agreed to help provide one for each of you. We're going to the store after dinner tomorrow night. They'll be waiting and we'll get what we need then. Later, I'll get to present the two of you to the audience and see how well you can do at raising a good bid from the crowd."

"But this isn't The Network," Tim objected. He was right. I wasn't going to argue with him. This was, in a very real way, a desecration of The Network and all it stood for. It was making fun of the serious intentions that he had. But it was something they were going to do, I had decided that.

"Consider it an exercise in humiliation," I told him. I reached out and took one of his nipples in my hand. "You can never have too much of that, after all."

"It's cruel," he said.

I pinched the tit as hard as I could between my nails. "There are many things that are cruel." When I let go, he was still glaring at me. "Go take a swim," I said. "If your swim suits are wet the other men will have a better look at your cocks. I want to study them while they watch you."

They moved more slowly than they ever had while they followed my instructions. But they did do it. They dove into the water and did laps up and down the cement pool. Around the edge there were dozens of eyes following as they made their trip back and forth. There was hunger in those eyes and there was enormous envy. I wanted to go up to the men who were doing nothing but watch and tell them they were the ones who were keeping themselves from knowing what was going on in life. They were the only reasons that they were on the sidelines. These boys might not be available to them, but there were so many who were. If you would only dare to do what Marc and Tim had finally done, each in his own way: Take the chance, risk, ask for help in releasing whatever is inside. But instead, there was only the crowd of people who would always be the on-lookers and never the actors.

An Interlude

The three of us swam and sunbathed for the rest of the afternoon. Marc and Tim got over their anxiety and reverted to their playful selves. They were freed by being here in the resort so far from home. Marc had been right, he was much more able to ease into the roles here than he would have been in New England.

Tim was reacting to it all as though it were a vacation. Yes, of course I would do things like tie that rawhide around his cock and balls and then leave it on while the heat of the sun shrank it and made the grip on his genitals even more tightly painful. But this was nothing compared to the highly ritualized life he had grown experienced to at home. There wasn't the constant labor and there wasn't the omnipresent possibility of some elaborate new form of sexual pleasure that I might devise for myself.

They were also renewing their own relationship. Tim liked nothing more than to have another slave to play with. It made him feel infinitely better to have someone to share the pleasure and the pain. He rose to the occasion whenever Marc was within hearing, just as he had whenever Sven had been closeby.

That wasn't a terribly unique form of slave mentality. It was a device that many used to turn their experiences into something of a bonding ritual with another bottom. *We can make it — together; I can do this if you help me* . . . Those were only some of the ways that the motivation showed itself in Tim and in others.

There was just the fact that they had been close at one time and had been separated. They had both had adventures which I know they were talking about together in ways they would rather not with me. There would be silly things that had happened to Marc in his trips to the city that he wouldn't want me to hear. And Tim would have his secret moments that he'd want to tell Marc about.

They would go into the pool, get money from me to buy a drink, sit just far enough away from me to be able to claim they were within distance to hear any request, but they would actually be beyond my ability to hear their whispers.

Through the whole afternoon their cocks were clear in their briefs and their balls pressed against the fabric. I entertained myself and the on-lookers by having them occasionally come and rub lotion on my body. The guest house was gay and I could take certain liberties here without any possible problem. My hand could rest on one of my young men's thighs, pinch a nipple, or feel a hard stomach.

I eventually took them back up to the room. My ideas for the slave auction and the sight of their near-naked bodies by the pool had gotten to me. With the slippery suntan lotion on our bodies, I had them climb on the bed. I dragged off their briefs and undid the rawhide. I was anxious for some play with them now; they'd had enough time with one another.

They were giggling and were more than willing to have something happen. I sent Tim off to get the condoms and lubricants from my bag.

"A nice start on a tan," I told Marc as I ran a hand on the white stripe around his middle. He was smiling at me with more than simply a hint of seduction.

I had taken off my own suit and stood in front of him with my half-hard cock near his face. He made a move towards it, expecting that the light manner I was using gave him that kind of permission. He might have been right, actually. That was certainly the signal I had given him. But I had better things in mind.

"Whoa!" I grabbed his head and kept him away from my cock. "A little more discipline here."

Before he understood what I was doing, I had taken a seat on the edge of the bed and was dragging his wonderful body across my lap. "Spread those legs!" I commanded. He stopped resisting then; the tone of my voice told him that I was getting more serious than he had realized. I reached over him and wrapped an arm around his midsection so I could grab hold of his cock and balls with it. His legs had obediently parted. I could see the whole inside of the crevice between his buttocks now with the small brown hole that had been shaved again that morning.

Tim was standing beside us with the things I had told him to get. "I think this one needs to remember his place better," I said to Tim. A broad smile came and his fine white teeth showed.

I ran a palm over both of Marc's asscheeks. The young flesh was so rubbery and resilient. It was cool from the recent swim in the pool. "Do you expect me to be satisfied with a cold fuck?" I was using a prankish tone of voice. Tim only smiled more; Marc tightened his buttock muscles. He knew perfectly well what was coming.

I lifted up my hand and brought it down hard onto the waiting ass. The room echoed the loud slap. I hit again, on the other side this time. "Just a little warm-up," I said jovially. My hand went back in the air and slammed home again.

Marc was trying not to show the effect this was having on him, but he couldn't help but move his ass. He was only trying to find some way to avoid the full brunt of the spanking that he knew was going to continue, but the effect was the opposite. He looked as though he was rotating his bottom like a happy hustler, actually asking for the next one.

Tim laughed at that. I simply enjoyed looking at it for a moment and then went on, finding more and more tender little spots on Marc's fine ass to leave a good, red imprint. By the end of it he was gripping hold of my legs and hiding his face in the covers. I could see from the movements of his shoulders that he was beginning to cry. My hand was stinging from the use and the surface of his buttocks was a uniform scarlet.

"Now, that's better," I said. I pushed him forward further on to the bed. He immediately separated his legs. The movement lifted up his midsection and the hairless anus was in perfect view again.

I crawled up between his thighs. My cock was hard. His own had been trapped by his upward motion and was pointing down, pressing from above by the mattress. Both his fine balls were stuck between his half erect cock and his body. I let my erection feel its way up and down his cleft. He shuddered when the tip of my shaft

125 &

would run around his hole. But he certainly wasn't trying to escape it, not even a little bit.

"Get me ready," I told Tim.

The other young man moved over beside us. He reached in and took a careful hold of my cock. He unwrapped one of the condoms and used it to sheath my erection. He took the lubricant then and smeared the the rubber with it.

I took my prepared cock and aimed it at Marc's ass. "This belongs to me know," I said, only half-aloud. "This is mine." I lunged forward and my cock was quickly ensnared in the smooth and hot inner flesh. Marc lifted up his back as the intrusion was being completed.

I pumped easily and joyfully at the fine ass, its hairless surface was my personal aphrodisiac. I could see it as its muscles were pumped up by his resisting position. It was such a fine ass. To think that I was going to be able to have it whenever I wanted . . . How I wanted . . . The way I wanted. . .

Tim had moved closer. I looked at him as he studied my fucking movements. He put his head down near us. He had been the receiver of this cock often in the past few months, but it still seemed to amaze him as he watched. He'd done the same thing when I used to fuck Sven.

He reached over and put a hand on top of Marc's buttocks. He could graze my erection as it moved in and out of Marc. He moved it only slightly, just enough to be able to feel the fall of my balls when I would dive into Marc's anus. When I lifted up, my testicles would also lift up away from his touch.

He moved a little and studied my face then. He was staring deeply into my eyes, as though he wanted the answer to a puzzle. Why did I want to do this to Marc? And why would other men want to do it to him? I somehow understood the question, but there was only one answer that I could conceive of giving him. I leaned down and kissed him on the lips.

I fought against letting myself go. I wanted to continue the fucking for the entire night. But the pressures were building up. I lifted up away from Tim's mouth, but then leaned back again in a slightly different way. He understood what I wanted and his lips came up and sucked in the closer nipple. One of his hands moved to the other. I closed my eyes in something close to ecstasy and threw my head back as I felt my cock gripped by Marc and my chest being manipulated by Tim. I pumped more quickly and even more violently, letting my belly slam against Marc's upturned buttocks.

Finally I yelled out and my cock seemed to send all of my body's fluids pulsing out of me and into the young man I had wanted for so long.

I collapsed on top of Marc. Tim moved to rub my back then. I let my erection subside. When it had, I pulled back my hips to let my cock escape from the hot hold of Marc's ass. I rolled off him to the edge of the bed.

Tim's cock was hard now. It was pointing straight up in the air. That was one of the things about it that I liked the most. It sometimes seemed as though it were flat against his belly when he was hard, even when he was standing.

I dragged him over to me. He seemed to expect that I was going to use my hand on him now. He went to assume the position to let me have that pleasure. But, instead, I stopped him. I sat him up on one of my knees. I took a nipple in my mouth and began to chew on it, just slightly. I took hold of his hard cock and began to pump it. He understood now what I was doing. I was simply going to masturbate him.

He responded by holding on to me tightly and pulling me against his neck. I could feel him kissing the top of my head. My one hand moved up and down the shaft and felt the drops of liquid that were escaping from the tip.

I have never been able to understand or communicate how much I adore men's cocks — that hard yet vulnerable flesh and the feel of the blood filling it up, the way their heads become so smooth-skinned when they're erect. I have always enjoyed the opportunity of having a young man climb up and let my hand grab his erection.

My ear was against Tim's chest and I could hear the building rhythm of his breathing. I let go of his nipple just long enough to say, "Yes," giving him encouragement and permission to orgasm. The cadence increased, the quickness of the expansion and contraction of his lungs picked up and then, in a moment that's always been miraculous to me, I felt the small geyser of come spill out onto my hand.

I looked up. His eyes were closed in his moment of relief. I kissed him. His eyes opened and he smiled, he kissed me back on the forehead. "You're not nearly as terrible as you want to make us think you are."

"No," I said, "I'm worse. And I'll prove it." I was full of mock severity now. "Marc, get over here. It's time you had the same treatment." I tossed Tim aside with a playful move and dragged Marc on to my lap. He was stiff from the show we had put on and from his body's memory of the recent fucking. There was still heat coming from his abused buttocks. I could feel it when I had him sitting on my thigh. But that seemed a distant memory now. I took his cock and smiled at him. "I'm going to show you how terrible I am." Then I bit lightly on his chest and started to pump his cock just as I had Tim's.

The Unexpected

Marc and Tim had hated the second visit to the leather store the next day. Sam and Joseph had been unrelenting in the attention they had paid the two younger men. Their hands had explored with even more audacity than they had the other day; after all, this time they had my explicit permission and it was also clearer just how much Marc and Tim had agreed to this sexual slavery.

The smiles that I'd gotten after the small bout of fucking and masturbation the previous afternoon were gone. So were the memories of Marc sliding against my body that night and being allowed to rub himself to orgasm on my side while we shared the double bed. I had been affectionate to Tim the next morning and had not only shaved his ass for him myself after his shower, but had taken the opportunity to explore that opening with my fingers and let him jerk off into the shower stall.

All those kindnesses were faint recollections in just a few hours. Instead I only had pouts and hurt looks. I decided to let them have their moment. I looked at the pile of purchases and borrowed merchandise we had gotten from the store and thought that the result would much more than adequately compensate for an afternoon by the side of the pool spent with sullen slave boys.

They hated the idea of the auction and the things that we'd gotten only made them loathe it more. As the hour approached, they retreated further and further into their individual minds. Too bad, I realized, because if they would have talked about it and if Tim had found that strength he always found when he shared an ordeal with another slave, they would have had a much easier time of it. If they wanted to forget all those learnings, it was not my problem.

Their petulance was almost amusing in the afternoon. In our room, while we were showering away the lotions and the heat of the sun, it became slightly annoying. I felt, at one point, like taking a belt to them and clearing the air. But I should never have underestimated the minds of slaves. They solved the problem in their own way and they did it without even being aware of how it happened.

I had dressed for dinner and was sitting with a cigarette and a cold drink while they were moving through the room. They weren't under the strictest discipline and I was allowing them to have small conversations. They would ask one another where a piece of clothing was, could Marc borrow a shirt of Tim's? That kind of roommate inquiry was flying around the small suite.

The auction wasn't until midnight. We were going to a fine restaurant that Joseph had recommended for dinner first. They were being allowed to leave the leather chaps and the SLAVE shirts behind. The chance to wear "civilian" clothing was a treat and they were reacting to it just that way.

In the course of it all, the items in the black paper bags began to be discussed. I hadn't gotten perfectly matched sets; there were some discrepancies in the uniforms. Somehow their talk moved from the color polo shirt each was wearing to which jockstrap would suit whom better later in the evening.

"Don't you want the belt with those diamond shaped studs?" Marc asked Tim at a certain point.

"I think it'd look better with that collar you wanted to wear."

I nearly missed the change in their attitude and almost broke in to point out the simple reality that I would be choosing their outfits for the auction. But I barely caught hold of myself in time to listen to the metamorphosis they were going through.

"Where can we put some of those chains? There are so many of them." Marc was going through one of the bags.

"Around our boots, like Sam does?" Tim wondered.

"That'd be good."

They bantered on like that for a few minutes. It was time to go. The three of us left the room and walked down the main street to dinner. I ordered for us and listened as the conversation moved even more into the evening's future events.

"I wonder how much money they're going to raise?" Tim asked. But he was really wondering how much he would bring at auction; it's the omnipresent concern of the slave to be sold. Who thinks he's worth how much?

"I know you'll get more than I will," Marc answered. He knew perfectly well what Tim was really saying.

"No, no," Tim responded. "I don't have your looks."

"But look at your body, they'll think you've been in a gym full-time for the whole past year."

Tim flexed an arm and studied it. "Gym? God, they should try just spending a week working at the house and they could save a fortune in expenses." They both thought that was humorous.

The whole tone changed. I tried to bring them back to their anger and concern. "What if Sam or Joseph buys you?"

Tim looked down at his plate. "I figure you're probably going to give me to them anyway, the way you've become so friendly." He didn't like the idea, but the firmly disciplined Tim was in control now, the one who understood that he was going to be sold into The Network. I saw, then, the Tim who might even be looking forward to the experience of being handed over to a master who was not his choice. This was one of the adventures he had been looking forward to, after all. Wasn't it?

Marc seemed to expect the same fate. "You're going to be doing it to me often enough, I guess. I should get accustomed to it." There was my first real indication that he was assuming that this vacation was going to work as much as I was.

"I just wish you'd . . . I just understand more things now," Tim said.

"Like what?"

He was playing with his dinner now. Finally he answered, "This is so much . . . less than what happened between Sven and you and me, isn't it? It's . . . common. This is the stuff that regular people do. I don't like it, all the clothes, it's so much less exciting than wearing Sven's gifts. I know now that it's one of the things you've been trying to teach us.

"Sven made that stuff for me. They're a special gift from a man who is as much my teacher in a way as you are. They're like a graduation gift. I hated them at first, you know that. They're so

131

small and their whole purpose is to leave me looking good for you — for my master — and to make me more . . . sensual.

"Isn't that the big part of it? It's what you're always saying, that so much of this is for us to learn how to be attractive for a master, to make our bodies more accessible to him?

"Instead, all the leather and chains and studs that we have to wear tonight make us look hard. It's different when we see those things on you. It turns me on — a lot. But it's armor, it's stuff to keep your body from someone else.

"I wasn't so sure about this trip. I knew it was really for Marc. But now I'm glad I'm doing it too." He looked at Marc then. "This was what you got at the leather bars, wasn't it? All the bottoms dressed up in their metal and being hard-assed and throwing attitude?"

Marc nodded agreement. "It was one of the problems I had. The ones who looked the best were the ones who didn't really want what I did. They were the ones who sent out some kind of signal of strength and promised more than anyone else. But they turned the whole thing into a match.

"I'd seen signs for slave auctions in the city bars, too. I never got to one, but I understood they'd be like tonight. The other most common event I saw advertised was wrestling matches. Why? I mean, that's fine, if people want to do that. But why were they such a regular fantasy for so many people?

"I asked around a bit and I learned that it was really just this whole big system that was an excuse for the bottoms. 'If I lose a match, then he can do anything he wants with me.' That's still all right, if someone wants it. But I kept running into the attitude that it was all there was. That was all those people could think of doing. It didn't make a whole lot of sense to me. Submitting to a man you choose makes much more." He looked at me and blushed.

Yes, yes, this was all going to work.

* * *

The bar was packed when we arrived. There was a *mardi gras* feel to the place. The patrons filled the entire spectrum of a gay bar: Leather and denim were expected, but the charity event had brought in men in suits, others in pressed cotton slacks and the younger ones who would be spending most of the season on the dance floor.

Marc and Tim looked around at the crowd and had a touch of nervousness about them. I led them to the back of the room and into the dressing area. Most of the other participants were already there. About a dozen men were drinking beer and a couple of them smoking joints. We were introduced around and then my two young men began to change.

As it was all going on, I could only wish that these other men's costumes were honest indications of their desires. There was one redhead with truly spectacular muscles who was wearing only a leather jockstrap and his boots. He would have been such a fine specimen on the real auction block, a real prize for his buyer in The Network. Here, he was only playing a game. The "good cause" had given him an excuse to show off his hard earned body. But his banter made it clear that he was more interested in the current voguish movies, than in casting himself in a supporting role himself.

There were also a pair of quite young men — no more than eighteen — who were going to present themselves in their underwear. They were clad only in bright white briefs and athletic stockings which covered their entire calves. They would have brought so much joy to a master who could have appreciated them. But they would be offered only to the ones in this common audience. I sighed, not really wanting to deny their purchasers the pleasures they would get tonight, but thinking of the unused potential the transactions would represent.

Not one of the men here really inspired me — other than my own two, who were quite something. They stripped down and began to get out the items that had been chosen and transported in duffle bags. They were much more at ease when they were naked than the other men expected. They made no move to either hide or expose themselves, but went about their work easily.

Marc pulled on a leather jock first. There were lines of small metal studs along the seams. Then he zipped on a pair of chaps. From the front, the effect was as though he had on a pair of leather pants, and the lines of white flesh that would show as he moved were small moments of personal pornography to me — and I'm sure the rest of the people who were watching him as well. It seemed that those glimpses of his bare thighs between the leather pieces were much more intimate than his total nudity had been.

His hairless torso was gleaming in the red light that came from

133 &

the backstage fixtures. It was a fine body, smooth and hard, with more than enough definition to satisfy even the most discerning onlooker. He took out the plain white t-shirt that he had so carefully torn earlier. When he dragged it down over his head the natural-looking holes left both of his nipples bare. There was a tear down the side, as well, that left a swatch of his stomach exposed.

He put his boots on over his thick socks next. The final touches were the chains. The two had decided that Marc should wear most of the pieces that had been accumulated. A particularly heavy length was looped around and around his right ankle. It wasn't the subtle signal of a masochist who would have a single strand on his boot at most. Marc's looked as though it had a substantial weight to it; he looked like a real slave, not a playmate. Another, shorter piece of chain went around his right bicep. Then a third was put through a belt loop on his right waist. It went underneath his crotch and back up his ass to the same section of his belt; finally the ends were allowed to hang from the waistband of the chaps.

Tim was also wearing chaps. But his jockstrap was the more usual white elastic material. It didn't cover up the lines of his genitals the way Marc's heavy leather codpiece did. On the contrary, the shape of his cock and balls would be apparent to every eye. He also wore a pair of heavy black boots. But there was no shirt. Instead, he wore only a leather vest. Tim's hairy chest would be an attraction in and of itself. There was no reason to hide the thick rug that covered the two big pectorals and then dove into a neat and thin line as it fell down his belly into the athletic supporter.

Rather than chains from his side, we snapped a pair of handcuffs to the belt loop. His right ankle was adorned with a pair of tit clamps and their metal chain. It was a subtle little message, I thought, and I hoped that someone in the audience would pick it up.

I was changing as well. The role of bar performer is hardly one to which I aspire. I almost never enter the places anymore. But the evening's activities were all in fun and I had decided to join. I had older, much more worn clothes than Marc and Tim. I already had on my black leather pants and my boots. They weren't the new and unused footwear that so many of the others had on, but Tim had polished them to a remarkably high sheen earlier in the day. He had really accomplished a great feat in his labor. Of course, he had done it with a riding crop in his mouth, a little hint as to the payment he'd make if the work hadn't been satisfactory.

I decided that I wouldn't wear a shirt either. I wore only my heavy leather jacket. I also had on my leather cap — the other two were to go hatless. On our way to the bar Marc had stopped at a store and seen something which he insisted I had to have as part of my gear: A pair of reflector sunglasses. In the spirit of the evening, I had gone in and bought them. I put them on now and the effect seemed to be quite impressive — at least from what I could see of the way my redheaded friend was reacting to me. A pair of leather gloves finished off the outfit and I felt ready for the event.

Outside this dressing area, the sounds of the night's entertainment were getting louder. The two youngsters in the jockey shorts had already gone on stage and had been greeted with yells and screams of delight. I could hear the voice of the master of ceremonies as he made rude and embarrassing comments on the pair. A sudden surge of sound indicated that the sale had been completed and the prizes were being delivered.

Marc and Tim were ready; they were dressed; they were waiting. I could only guess what was going through their minds. Tim had to be imagining the scene at The Network. This is what it would be. I would have to convince him that it wasn't so, this wasn't even a hint of it. The fear he might be feeling now about walking out onto that stage was nothing compared to what would surge through his body when he was presented in the chambers of The Network. The slight anxiety of being humiliated in front of a crowd of strangers and then being sent off with one unknown person and being expected to perform a few sexual favors was meaningless compared to the sudden realization that years of his life were going to be decided for him in the hour or two of The Network auction. Still, I knew I could use tonight to help him get ready for the real thing.

Marc was just as shocked. These were the things he had thought about and dreamed of for so long. These were the acts that he had gone to cities to search out and had been so disappointed in. He stared at me quickly, as though he understood now just how much we were going to be doing together and how much we would mean to one another. He was here with me and his friend and he was doing these things. How could he? How could he have even crossed the line when it was cushioned by the thousands of miles of distance from his home? And what did it mean to him? Would he go backwards? Could he? Did he want to? Those questions must have been coursing through his thoughts.

More men left the dressing room and went on to the stage as their names were called. We were to be the last. The organizer had been so taken with the possibilities that we represented that we were to be the stars of his little event. The redhead was the only other one left. I watched as he studied each of the three of us. His tongue would come out and wet his lips. Who did he want? I wondered. But the way he would look at my gloved hands while I smoked a cigarette gave away his desires.

"Let's get ready," I said to Marc and Tim. They moved towards me cautiously. The sounds of the full house of the bar were getting louder. They knelt in front of me. I reached into the closer of the two duffle bags and found the two leather collars that I had put there. I pulled them out and attached one to each young man's neck. I got out the leashes that matched the collars and attached them.

The redhead was entranced with all of it. He was studying the two young men and I swore he was debating joining them on their knees. I looked at him and wondered if he'd dare ask. But someone came and beckoned him on to the stage. He'd be next. I pulled at my leashes and Tim and Marc fell to their hands and knees and followed me to the edge of the stage so we could watch.

My interested and anxious redhead was clowning now, he'd left behind those hints of submission when he'd walked out in front of the crowd. His hands were thrown up in the air, as though he were a victor and not someone being sold. The image he presented now was much, much less interesting than what I had seen earlier. The small picture of his tiny tongue moving over his lips had been a hint of something that might have intrigued me. This was the usual boorishly macho image of the gay bar.

The men in the audience made lewd comments to him as the master of ceremonies theatrically pinched one of his tits and he recoiled from the slight contact. "Fine slave," someone joked with a demeaning intent. I agreed. What a sham of decent manhood that he would react to such a little thing as fingers on his nipples? He had clearly been dreaming of so much more in our moments of silent communication.

Then he turned around and showed off his ass. It was not bad, not bad at all. The master of ceremonies gave it a good slap and the redhead at least didn't recoil this time. The crowd laughed again. The redhead played to them a bit, mimicking one weightlifter's pose to display his considerable biceps and then another to show off his substantial chest.

The bidding began. I hadn't actually seen it before and I was interested. Even though they were on their knees beside me, I knew that Marc and Tim were also studying it. It was in straight cash sums; all of it would go to the charity. The bids began at very small amounts. But that seemed to be on purpose, to allow many different men a sense that they were really taking part in the activities. The final offers were quite generous and seemed to be coming from only a few individuals. The lights were so bright that I couldn't make out any of their features. Only a few people right at the edge of the stage could be easily seen from where I stood.

Then the master of ceremonies was announcing the final opportunities to bid. "Going, going. . ." Something seemed to grip my chest. I hadn't expected that. I drew in a deep breath.

There was one final yell from the crowd and then the redhead disappeared into the mass of men. We were next. The master of ceremonies made an introduction. Two men were going to be presented next, he said. These were the ones he expected the highest bids on. There was little, he implied, that couldn't be done to these "real" slaves so long as the purchaser stayed within the confines of health. Tim was startled to hear those words spoken. He knew I had to have given permission. He must have been shocked to understand that any stranger was being told that he and Marc were even more available for even more acts than the rest of the men had been. But it was too late to object or protest — neither of which would have done him any good.

I tugged at their leashes and led the two crawling men onto the stage. A roar went up from the crowd even louder than any before. There was a round of applause. They were getting more from the three of us than they had from any of the others. We weren't awkward and we weren't acting stupidly in response to this auction. There were two of the best looking males in the room, their asses naked in the frame of their chaps. My hold on their leads was more than an act and that must have been apparent to at least some of them.

I took the two young men to the center of the stage and then pulled up on the leashes sharply enough that Marc actually let his hands fly to his neck to protect it. He sheepishly caught himself and, to the enjoyment of many of the onlookers, dropped his hands back to his side. They thought they were ready for the sale, but I had made other arrangements. I reached into my pockets and took out two sets of tit clamps. The audience roared again as they saw me place one of the devices on each of the male's bodies.

Now we were ready. The master of ceremony began with Marc. He was petrified by the whole thing. He looked out into the crowd with a wild expression on his face that left his fear naked to anyone who would look at him. The sums bid for him began to climb quickly. I walked behind him, never letting up on my grip on his leash or on Tim's. I reached down and took hold of the torn t-shirt and pulled hard to rip away almost all of it. Only a few strips hung onto the neck. The crowd went wild and a new wave of bids came in.

I knelt and reached in front of him. I whispered an obscenity into his ear, a promise of something I planned to do to him. He rubbed the side of his face against mine. I was playing with the cup of his codpiece and the combination of the erotic words and the physical touch was too much. It overcame his stage fright. His cock was lengthening and the tip crept up over the top of the leather. Someone in the crowd saw it and yelled to the rest of them to see what was going on. The size of his erection proved to be still another selling point. There was a further wave of offers.

I stood up and moved so that my leather-covered crotch was resting on the top of his head. There were more jeers and even more bids. Then, finally, the master of ceremonies announced the close of the auction. "Going, going..."

A hammer hit the lectern he was standing behind and there was a round of applause for the lucky winner. I undid the leash to Marc's collar and stood him up. I gave him a kiss and slapped his bare ass to send him running off the stage and into the arms of his transient master.

Then I went to Tim. I knelt beside him, just as I had with

Marc. I whispered into his ear too, but my message was different. "So you want to be sold to The Network," I said, my voice dripping with sarcasm. "And you want to have your contract bought. Then you might as well get used to it and take advantage of the practice. Let's see you show them some good reason to put out good money for you. What are you going to offer in exchange? These men are only after a good time for an evening. Can you show them you're worth it? If you can't, how do you expect to have someone in The Network believe that you are going to be worth any considerable sum?"

My lecture enraged him. He knew perfectly well that I didn't even believe it all myself. This wasn't The Network. This was a gay bar full of men, almost all of whom were just acting silly. But I had given him a challenge and he was going to meet it.

He threw out his chest, pushing aside the vest and making sure that everyone could see the rubber-tipped clamps that were attached to his flesh. His arms went behind his back. He moved from side to side to make sure that they all got a good look at him. He did it all quite well, I thought. But the best moment came while the master of ceremonies was introducing him and making a jest about his "good training." As soon as it had been said, Tim leaned over and kissed each of my boots with a delicate and graceful gesture that didn't bring a yell from the crowd, but a moment of embarrassed silence. A lot of them suddenly understood that Tim and I meant these things to be serious.

The master of ceremonies broke into the awkwardness and began the auction. It went just as quickly as Marc's had. There were some men here who obviously were taken with Tim's body hair and with the very simple fact of the tit clamps. I heard remarks that proved that. I helped them along by lifting up the chain between the two clamps and pulling it enough that they could all see pieces of Tim's flesh pulled away from his torso.

The bidding war picked up even more. Tim seemed to want to put in his part as well. Or else he was trying to say something to me. He moved over and ran his tongue up and down the leg of my leather pants. The crowd went wild one more time.

When the master of ceremonies was making his final statements, "Going, going. . . ." the price was the highest it had been for any sale all evening. I joined in the applause this time and sent Tim on his way to the buyer. The lights had kept any of us from seeing those faces back in the crowd. He couldn't possibly have known what the man would be like. I could only imagine the terror in his mind as he ran through the bodies that were pushing him to the goal they knew, even if he didn't.

The master of ceremonies and I shook hands and started to walk off the stage. The event was over. But then there was cry from the crowd. *"Sell the master!"* I took it as a joke and waved back as we kept on moving. "Yes, sell the master," another man yelled. The idea was infectious. Even before we could leave the stage, it seemed as though the whole audience had taken it up.

The master of ceremonies grabbed my arm and said, "Why not?" I stared at him. I had no intention of allowing this to go on. I tried to take my arm out of his grip, but he kept on talking, "It's for a good cause and you're what they want right now. Come on, your friends did it."

The audience took our hesitation as agreement and the applause was thundering. I gave in. It was only a joke, I reminded myself. I was being sold as a "master" and while that might offend me, this was simply a resort community. This was — as I had told Marc and Tim — a break in the intensity of our lives in the mountains. Why not...

Why not, indeed. I stood in the center of the stage. I refused to posture, but my natural stance with my hands on my belt was more than satisfactory for the crowd. There was a continual flow of lewd remarks about the shape of my genitals in my pants, questions about the worth of a bid for the sake of getting hold of the prize inside. The master of ceremonies began with a lecture, reminding the men that this was a different sale altogether. He teased them by saying that they should remember that they needed to question more than whether they could afford the cost, they had to wonder if they could afford the consequences of winning the auction.

There were loud guffaws and more clapping. And then it started. The lights were what set it off in my mind. They blinded me the moment I took off my dark glasses. I couldn't see the faces of the crowd. They were all anonymous. That was the beginning. Then the jokes, the crude remarks — this wasn't the closed world of The Network; this wasn't a study in elegance; there was no safety in its ritual.

I was there — in The Network. I could only vaguely bring myself back to this place and realize that the master of ceremonies had begun the bidding on me. 'They are bidding on a master,' I reminded myself. But the memories were too powerful, they were too intense. I looked down at the lights that shone up from the edge of the stage to blind me. Instead I saw a mirrored surface. It was years ago. I wasn't dressed in leather and I didn't have on any glasses to hide the expression of my eyes. I was naked, kneeling on a mirrored table...

Now — in my mind — the faces came into focus and they filled me with fear. I saw them — the men and the women of all races. There were Asians whose long nails clawed delicately at my chest and Africans whose intentions were as primeval as the forests they came from. Then there was a woman, a gorgeous woman with full skirts and fine make-up who lingered so long in front of my table that I was sure that she would be the one.

But she wasn't. I knew who it would be when he was standing there. He was tall and substantial looking. He put a hand on my cheek and lifted my head up to look at me more closely. There was nothing to hide behind on that day. That day was so long ago, but this act of being here on this stage made me remember all the little details.

The master of ceremonies was shouting out to repeat the bids that came from the audience. I looked at him and barely comprehended what he was doing. It was so insignificant compared to that day so many years ago when a much more august auctioneer had held my fate in his hands. His sale had been silent, communicated only with the hand motions of the guests who sat in regal and silent comfort while the proceedings went on. When they were over, I was the one who was taken from the stage — but not in leather finery to make me look more like a fantasy of one of these men in a crowded bar. Oh, no, I was taken naked and totally, utterly vulnerable to that man, that one man who...

"Going, going, gone!" The hammer went down on the lectern and I was standing there, sold. I was dripping perspiration. It was gluing my body hair to the lining of the leather jacket. I couldn't quite get myself back together. The memories were still coming so strongly that I wasn't back here in the bar yet.

I was stunned. How could memories be forced so far back in one's consciousness and then be so suddenly released? I hadn't really thought of that evening where I'd been introduced to The Network with that much detail in years. Now, on the stage, it had forced itself to the forefront of my mind. I had to get away from it and return...

"So you're my master," the man said. He had climbed up on the stage to claim his prize. Joseph. I smiled at him. He put an arm around my shoulders and we climbed down off the stage.

Unwritten Chapters

Tim got back to the room before Marc. I was glad, I wanted some time alone with him. He smiled when he saw me in the bed. "Come here," I said. He walked over to me. I reached up and gently drew him onto the mattress. I wrapped my arms around him and kissed him. He was startled at first, but soon his arms came up and embraced me.

"Get undressed," I whispered into his ear.

He jumped off the mattress and took off the leather clothing from last night's auction. I stripped too. Now we both climbed under the covers. I carefully rolled him onto his back and then climbed on him. He obediently spread his legs to accommodate my hardening cock. I kissed him more, enjoying the sensation of having my whole torso laid out on his hairy flesh. I lifted myself up on my elbows so I could look down onto his face. He was staring back, a little puzzled, but obviously pleased.

I reached over to the nightstand and got out a condom and lubricant. He started to reach for them, but I stopped him and unraveled the latex onto my erection and greased it up myself. Then I once again pressed my weight onto him. His legs moved up and around my waist to give me easy access. I took advantage of the position and let my cock move against the ring of muscle that guarded his anus.

I slipped past and into the warm insides. I moved my hips carefully and luxuriously. I let myself — and him — enjoy a slow, casual fuck. My whole length would slide back and forth, drawing the most intense reactions from him. There was no assault in this; this was love-making and he seemed to understand that from the very beginning.

I kept on kissing him, letting my lips move from his forehead to his mouth, then over his cheeks and down to his neck. I still had my elbows supporting me and I could run my hands through his thick hair. I played with his beard, never pulling it or tugging it the way I might have another time, but letting my fingers weave their way through its strands, even sucking on the wiry hair at one point.

He wasn't in control of his reactions to the strong, deliberate fucking I was giving him. His legs would move with quick jerks, then they'd pull me into him like the arms of a vise. His hands tried to simply rest on my shoulders, but the constant pumping of my hips made him clutch hold of me at times. After a number of minutes, he was kissing me wildly. I kept back my orgasm and simply kept it up. I wanted him to remember this. There wasn't going to be another one like it in a long time.

I rolled him onto his side so I could reach my head down and suck in one of his nipples. He froze, preparing for my teeth to attack his delicate tits. But I only played with them with my lips, my tongue was all that ran over the sensitive surface. The new contact made him even more frenzied.

My hands were on the sides of his buttocks. I began to move them. One came around to wedge itself between our bellies and find his hard cock. I played with it gently. All the time that I kept up that insistent fucking, I ran my fingertips over the surface of his erection. I started to grip his cock harder and make my manipulations more intense only when I knew that I couldn't hold either one of us back much longer.

I picked up the tempo of my fucking then. I moved more quickly and my actions let him know I was close to coming. I kissed him full on the mouth and our tongues played with each other. My hand was driving him further and further while our bellies slapped against each other. When we came it was as close to perfectly timed orgasms as I think I've ever known. Just as my cock was pulsing against the walls of his ass, his own was sending waves of hot fluid out of its slit onto both our stomachs.

It was over. A whole lot of things were over. I gently pulled out of him. He was sprawled on his back on the mattress, one arm was over his head. He was clearly exhausted. He was also impressed. His eyes had a slight glaze to them. We hadn't had that kind of sex before — ever.

I didn't say anything. I got out of the bed and went into the bathroom and showered. He joined me in a very short time. He must have expected more of the same affection. But I ignored him. He began to soap up my body as he had so often in the past. He moved languidly over my chest and shoulders. Then, with a move he clearly didn't expect, I pushed him onto his knees. The stream of water from the showerhead was raining down on him. He looked up at me, almost shocked. But the intent was obvious. He lathered my genitals and then his hands washed my thighs, my calves and finally my feet.

I turned around and he went over the whole bottom half of my body from the rear. I could feel him washing my ass and the backs of my knees. When he was done I rinsed off and stepped out of the stall.

He came right after me. His eyes were red from having been in the path of the shower for so long. But I didn't say a thing. I stood there and he realized I expected him to dry me off. He took one of the big bath towels and went about his work silently. There was an obvious expression of anger mixed with confusion on his face. He didn't understand the sudden transformation I'd gone through.

Then I went into the bedroom and got dressed. He came out after he'd wiped himself dry and stood there awkwardly. "Get some clothes on," I said. He nodded and got out a pair of jeans and a t-shirt. When he had them on I sent him down to the lobby to fetch a cup of coffee for me. He came back with two; one was obviously supposed to be for him. I took one of the cups and poured it out the window. He stared at me in disbelief. But I think he understood at that moment that we'd come to an important milestone in his training. It was time for us to prepare for the end.

I took one of the comfortable chairs and he knelt by my side while we waited. Marc wasn't much longer. I had just finished drinking my coffee when he came through the door. I stood up and met him, giving him a kiss and a strong hug to welcome him.

"You smell good. Have your already showered?"

"Yes," he said.

"Fine. Just jump into some street clothes and we'll go out. I don't think the villagers are ready for your bare ass in the morning."

"Okay." He turned and said something in greeting to Tim who was still kneeling by the chair. The other young man didn't answer, but only stared at the floor. Marc didn't seem to notice, or else didn't take it seriously. Perhaps he thought that he'd walked into one of our discipline sessions. He simply pulled off the auction clothes and got into an outfit much like Tim's — jeans and a t-shirt and running shoes.

The three of us left the room and walked onto the main street. "What was your night like?" I asked Marc.

"It was fine. Very uneventful. The guy wasn't unattractive, but he wasn't into much either. He was more intrigued than anything else, I think. He liked the leather and asked me to keep it on when we got back to his house. He didn't really want to do much of anything. I think he was embarrassed about the circumstances. It had all seemed pretty hot to him at the bar, but when he was faced with a stranger he couldn't follow through. We talked for a long time and we went to bed. He did ask me to sleep with just the chaps on — I thought that was hot. When I was almost asleep he reached over and began to play with me and with himself. He ended up jerking us both off.

"This morning — like so many of the tricks I've had before — he couldn't even talk about it. He made me breakfast and got very worried about me walking through town with nothing over my behind. He made me promise I'd take some back streets to get home." He laughed. He liked the story.

"You? I saw you and Joseph go off together. What happened?"

"A lot of things — not that much sexual. We talked a great deal. I had a chance to think through what I'm doing and what's happening between us."

"That sounds heavy."

I had to admit that I'd spoken with a very portentous tone. Before Marc had a chance to say anything else — and before he could notice that Tim hadn't taken any part in our conversation — I led them into one of the fine gift shops.

The clerks were helpful as we walked through the store. I kept asking Marc what he thought of various potential purchases. Did he think this clock would look good in my study? What about these candlesticks in the living room? I wasn't terribly surprised when he fell right into the conversations. I had even — after last night's introspection — expected him to.

We ended up with a pile of boxes. The pleased shopkeeper took my credit card and processed the sale while one of his helpers put our things in two large bags. When it was all completed, the clerk passed the bags over the counter. Marc went to take one of them. I stopped him. "Tim will carry them."

He was startled, but wasn't going to argue with me. We kept on with our shopping. After that time in the first shop, I watched carefully to see what assumptions both young men would make. It was uncanny. I had predicted everything perfectly. Tim never spoke a single word for the next two hours. He glowered for a while, but then seemed to fall into his role of porter, quickly and efficiently taking the parcels. At one point I told him to run back to the guest house and unload the armful he had accumulated. He did it and, when he caught up with us again, he was out of breath — he had actually run the whole distance.

One of the last stops was a men's wear shop, one of the most stylish in the South. We passed the underwear section and I stopped at one display. Marc came up and stood beside me. There was a whole collection of silk garments. "We should buy some for you. It'll make you feel more erotic. The fabric will cling to you and caress you. You still have a lot to learn about becoming more voluptuous. This could help you."

"You just want to feel it on me," he joked.

"Of course I do," I answered. "You should know that by now. Which styles should we buy? Which colors?" We went through the selection and I ended up taking a half-dozen assorted pair to the counter.

"But you've only bought one of each," Marc said. "What about Tim?"

"Tim won't have any use for any of this," I said.

Over lunch I explained that this was our last day. I'd already booked our passage back to New England. That was the reason for the spree. I hadn't expected either one to argue, and neither did.

When we got back to the room, they went about packing. We ate our dinner — one of those packaged abominations — on the jet as it flew north.

I drove the car from the Boston airport in complete silence. They didn't speak either — as much from fatigue as anything else, I think, though they both had to have questions and thoughts about my actions.

When we got to the house in the mountains, I walked in first. I had left the heat on very low, only high enough to keep the pipes from freezing. It was cold inside. I went to the fireplace where wood was already laid out and took a match to start the flame going.

Marc and Tim came in soon after, each with his arms loaded with luggage and other packages. I stood up and told Marc to stay with me. Tim was to get the rest of our things out of the car. I took a seat on the couch and Marc came and sat beside me. I put an arm around his shoulder and he leaned into me. There were occasional noises as Tim came in and out of the doorway.

"I have it all," he finally said. He was standing in the doorway looking at the homey scene that Marc and I must have composed.

"Why are you in those clothes?" was my only response.

"It's cold." I could tell from the petulant sound of his voice that he knew he'd made a mistake.

"First of all, strip. Then go and unpack all of our things. When you're done, bring a leather paddle downstairs so I can punish you for your insolence."

"Yes, sir."

Marc started to get up. He already had a hand on his top shirt button. He obviously expected that the order referred to him as well.

"Stop," I said.

"Aren't I just a slave too?" He was angry and there was a hint of defiance in the way he sat.

"No. Actually, you're not. You agreed to take a vacation and to try certain things. That was the limit to what we had decided. The trip is over and so are your obligations."

I went over to the bar and poured each of us a drink. I brought them back to the couch and handed him his.

"Then what happens now?" he asked.

"We can make an arrangement, or we can end it all."

"Just like that," he said.

"There aren't a great number of options now."

"What are you offering me?"

I turned and looked at him, wondering just what he meant.

He seemed to understand my confusion. "You've always said that The Network contracts gave the slaves some things — money, at least."

"That's true," I said. "I'm prepared to put you through college. I'll cover all the expenses. In addition, I'll deposit money in a savings account for you every month that you remain here in this house." I mentioned a specific sum which seemed more than adequate. "In return, you'll agree to provide any and all sexual services I request . . . "

"Including the sadistic ones?"

"Yes. Including the sadistic ones in all ways. I expect you to dress as I tell you to, spend your time only as I approve of it, travel with me when I desire."

"And if there's a . . . 'friend' who wants me, you'll expect me to go with him, just as I did at the resort after the auction?"

"Yes. I could add that it will happen very, very infrequently. But that would have to be a part of the agreement."

"How long will this last?"

"Quite possibly for the rest of our lives."

"Just like that? We're going to be lovers?"

"We've started falling in love already, haven't we?"

"Probably a long time ago — at least we started a long time ago."

"I'm only asking you to admit that it's happening."

"And you think that it will happen more easily and more effectively if we structure everything this way?"

"I underestimated you, Marc. I wasn't sure you understood that part of it. But, yes, I think we'll fall in love more easily if we start this way."

"How can we? You aren't falling in love with Tim."

"Aren't I? I think I am. But in a totally different way."

"Then, this . . . relationship of ours could change? It might not stay this way?"

"I strongly doubt we'll ever put a white picket fence around the house, if that's what you're asking. For now, you're young and inexperienced. You've proven that you are perfectly capable of not facing many things in your life and of messing up many others. For the next few years you're going to put your life in my hands and I'm going to see if I can't do a decent job of getting you going in certain directions. In return, you're going to give me a kind of sexuality that I want.

"When this chapter is over, then we'll have to renegotiate."

"But you do admit there's a time when that will happen?"

"Yes. I know it will. There are going to be a lot of things that will happen in the time to come."

"Is this the stuff that you learned while we were away?"

"Some of it." I didn't want to discuss too much of that. There were still parts of my conversation with Joseph that were painful to recall. "I was remembering all that's happened to me over the years and all the alterations my life has gone through." That was as much as I wanted to admit now.

"I don't understand," he pressed. "What could happen to change how you want me?"

"How you want to be." That was the key. I turned and looked at him carefully. "You're young. This might not be the place you'll stay. You're going to pay for the education you're going to receive in the next few years — trust me, you're going to pay. And I don't mean the college diploma that you're going to receive from it. That's one of the most minor points, in fact.

"Your education is a series of lessons in sexuality that hardly any people ever receive in this world. Living in this house is going to expose you to options of erotic life that you've never dreamt about. You can't know how you'll react to them all now. It may take years for you to understand the many attractions. But you're going to have the opportunity to explore.

"I'm going to be your guide. That's why you're going to have to put so much faith in all of my decisions. I'm going to take you on a tour of the senses that you couldn't even map out for yourself. When it's done? Well, if we're both honest and we're both intent on the learning that you have to do, we'll undoubtedly be in love. But it might not mean that you'll be here with me when it's over — at least not in the way we're going to start."

"You're going to be my Network."

"No. In fact, that's one of the things I've realized. The Network is totally different. Anyone who enters it does it all alone. There is the constant threat that other forces will intrude and change the location, the cast of characters, the action — all of it. There is no control and there is no constant in The Network. That's why what's going to happen to you and to Tim will be so totally different.

"I'm offering you a life with me where the outcome isn't settled. It could go in many different directions. Tim won't have your security and he won't have your options. He can hope for companionship on his road, but there's no assurance he's going to get it.

"I allowed him to have Sven. I even allowed him to have you while you were being introduced to so many things. But this is the end of your friendship with him. It's the beginning of your life with me — if you want it — and the start of the final phase of his education."

At that moment, Tim appeared in the doorway. He was naked. The leather paddle was in his hand. He looked at me and then at Marc with a slight sense of fear. That same fear had made his cock half hard. It hung heavily down from his body. He was going to do very well in The Network.

The furnace had been turned on, but it hadn't really warmed up the house yet. There were bumps on Tim's skin, visible even through the thick body hair.

"Kneel down facing the fire," I said calmly. "Put your forehead on the floor, spread your legs and lift up your ass."

He moved quickly to do what I said. The paddle was left on the floor beside him. It wasn't fear that was making him shiver now, it was the anticipation.

"Marc, pick up the paddle."

Marc looked at me for a brief moment and seemed to hesitate. But then he stood up and went and got the paddle. He was standing beside the naked, kneeling figure.

"Beat him."

Marc looked at the leather in his hand and then down at the young man who only a few months ago was his roommate. I wondered if he remembered just how intensely important it had been to Tim that other slaves and he not be separated. But now these two were being divided into starkly different classes.

Marc gripped the leather handle and then let it fall on Tim's waiting buttocks. "Harder! It's not a sign of affection. He failed his duties."

The leather went through the air again and this time it landed with a resounding slam. "That's more like it," I said. He lifted up the paddle again and delivered another blow. Then a third.

It took about six before he made Tim cry out. Then another half dozen before he was in tears. I wouldn't let Marc stop until I could hear the sobs.

"Tim, get a sleeping bag out of the closet. From now on, you're to stay at the foot of the bed at night. Only Marc will be sleeping with me. You're to consider him a master over you and fulfill every one of his requests quickly — if not, you'll be punished.

"You," I said to Marc, "are to use him as you want. Take advantage of the next couple of months. It may be a long time before you're able to have this chance with another man. He's going into The Network. He's no longer another guy who's going to have his sexuality with a partner in privacy and he's no longer the man who you knew for years. He's different — he's chosen to be different. If you spare that paddle, if you let him forget what his mouth and ass are for, if you let him think that life can be some little game, you'll only do him a disservice.

"He's committed himself to a certain path and anything that lets him forget that is not a kindness. Not at all."

* * *

It took them a month, really, to accept what had happened and how it all changed their relationship. Marc was like the unsophisticated customer who can't accept the gracious attention of a waiter in a fine restaurant at first. He'd apologize for making requests. He'd put his desire in the most ambiguous language. He wouldn't really be able to pull back far enough to make himself comfortable with the idea of someone serving him.

It was especially difficult because he was having to have to learn my desires at the same time. He was caught between the two roles — both of them my demands. He was to learn his place in relation to me, and at the same time he was to take part in Tim's training.

They were so uncomfortable at the start that they would occasionally break into smiles. I took care of that soon enough. It wasn't fair to punish Marc when it happened. It also invited him to take an escape route that would make him feel better: He could take the abuse and think he was being noble by doing that rather than disciplining Tim himself. I solved it by declaring that Tim would always have to assume the responsibility for any falling short they did.

It only took one session with Tim under a lash to convince Marc that he was doing his old friend no good by not demanding service.

But Marc didn't really have to do that much. Tim, it turned out, was the one who understood that this was the time he had to use to prepare himself. He had his last contact with the "real world" taken away from him — Marc. And to make it all the more emphatic, he had to live in my house with that same person constantly reminding him that a line had been crossed.

His passage wasn't yet irrevocable, but it was getting very close to that and he knew it. It was — finally — the most important lesson I had to give him. Here was his old friend, now being groomed to take over the duties of running the household. Tim had no choice but to accept this new ruler in addition to myself.

He threw himself into it. I would pass by a doorway and overhear a conversation: "No, you should make me do that." Or: "Just tell me, please, don't ask."

The final proof came sexually. They had permission — even orders — to have sex. I came across the bedroom one day and could spy on them inside it without their knowledge. I watched as Marc asked for sex. He didn't make the request with any sense of power at all. But, as I watched, Tim walked over to him and knelt down with a movement of astonishing grace.

I recognized it as one that he'd seen Sven accomplish many times. On his knees, before he even moved to put on Marc's condom, Tim's hands went to the side of his loincloth and untied it so it fell to the floor. He did it in a way that seemed to show that he shouldn't have any clothing on when he was about to serve a master.

Marc saw the action and put a hand on Tim's head. It seemed

as though he was really trying to comfort him. But Tim took the action in a manner that a slave would, as a gesture of great kindness from a lord. He moved into the hand as it stayed by his face and I could see him kiss it.

Only after all of these fine gestures did Tim take a condom and carefully — almost reverently — put it on Marc's now hard cock. When it was stretched over the erect flesh, Tim moved forward and kissed it gently. Only then did he open his mouth and let the whole of it slide in.

I watched them while they went through the entire sex act together. I saw the way that Tim's throat struggled to keep all of Marc inside. I carefully looked at the wonderful way that Marc's hip muscles worked as they pumped at Tim. They were quite beautiful with one another.

I watched to see if there was any sign that Marc would have the indications, the inclinations...

But I didn't see them — yet. I wondered. I wondered what would happen to him. In the years ahead it might be that he and I would go together to an auction to find some slave who would have to satisfy us both. Or it might be that I would have to take Marc there, myself, and leave him.

The thought hurt. It was foolish of me. Those were things in the far, far future. He had so much to learn and I had so much to learn about him.

I wondered how this next stage of my life would work. I now had Marc. There was so much that would happen to us. I had little idea what it would be. If I had bought a slave at auction, I would have known — I would have been certain what the outcome would be. But that hadn't happened. I had insisted on having my own story.

Now, I would have to wait to have it unfold. I had done this before — when I had climbed on a mirrored glass table years ago and hadn't known what could possibly come next.

So, all three of us were waiting for our chapters to be written. Marc and I here, in my house in the mountains. And Tim, who would soon know what it felt like to be naked on a leash, being led on hands and knees, towards a line of glass tables...

Other books of interest from
ALYSON PUBLICATIONS

SAFESTUD, by Max Exander, $8.00. At first, Max Exander thinks safe sex is a disappointment. But he gradually discovers that the change can be exciting in surprising and invigorating ways.

I ONCE HAD A MASTER, by John Preston, $9.00. In this collection of erotic stories, John Preston outlines the development of an S/M hero.

ENTERTAINMENT FOR A MASTER, by John Preston, $9.00. John Preston continues the exploration of S/M sexuality that he began in *I Once Had a Master.* This time, the Master hosts an elegant and exclusive S/M party.

THE LOVE OF A MASTER, by John Preston, $8.00. After the elegant S/M party in *Entertainment for a Master,* what more could the Master desire? Well, certainly not a return to the quiet life. Perhaps he could discover dark sexual yearnings in one of the hunky young men around him who just might be searching for the *Love of a Master.*

BELOW THE BELT AND OTHER STORIES, by Phil Andros, $8.00. Phil Andros, the narrator and intrepid hustler, follows the lead of his superb natural endowments, street smarts, and lively curiosity toward their inevitable tangled ends.

MACHO SLUTS, by Pat Califia, $10.00. Pat Califia has put together a stunning collection of her best erotic short fiction. She explores sexual fantasy and adventure in previously taboo territory.

STUD, by Phil Andros, $7.00. Phil Andros is a hustler with a conscience, pursuing every form of sex — including affection — without apology.

VAMPIRES ANONYMOUS, by Jeffrey McMahan, $8.00. Andrew, the wry vampire, was introduced in *Somewhere In the Night,* which won the author a Lambda Literary Award. Now Andrew is back, as he confronts an organization that has already lured many of his kin from their favorite recreation, and that is determined to deprive him of the nourishment he needs for survival.

STEAM, by Jay B. Laws, $10.00. A vaporous presence is slowly invading San Francisco. One by one, selected gay men are encountering it — then they disappear, leaving only a ghoulish reminder of their existence. Will anyone be able to stop this shapeless terror?

THE ADVOCATE ADVISER, by Pat Califia, $9.00. Whether she's discussing the etiquette of a holy union ceremony or the ethics of zoophilia, Califia's advice is always useful, often unorthodox, and sometimes quite funny.

DOC AND FLUFF, by Pat Califia, $9.00. When Doc, "an old Yankee peddler" with a big bike, leaves a wild biker party with Fluff (a cute and kinky young girl), she doesn't know that Fluff is the property of the bike club's president. Trouble — and sexy adventure — follow.

THE GAY BOOK OF LISTS, by Leigh Rutledge, $8.00. A fascinating and informative collection of lists, ranging from history (6 gay popes) to politics (9 perfectly disgusting reactions to AIDS) to useless (9 Victorian "cures" for masturbation).

LAVENDER LISTS, by Lynne Y. Fletcher and Adrien Saks, $9.00. *Lavender Lists* starts where *The Gay Book of Lists* and *Lesbian Lists* left off! Dozens of clever and original lists give you interesting and entertaining snippets of gay and lesbian lore.

COMING TO POWER, edited by SAMOIS, $10.00. A collection of writings and graphics, this book helped break the silence surrounding the issue of S/M in the lesbian and feminist movements.

THE MEN WITH THE PINK TRIANGLE, by Heinz Heger, $8.00. Thousands of gay people suffered persecution at the hands of the Nazi regime. Of the few who survived the concentration camps, only one ever came forward to tell his story. This is his riveting account of those nightmarish years.

WORLDS APART, edited by Camilla Decarnin, Eric Garber, Lyn Paleo, $8.00. The world of science fiction allows writers to freely explore alternative sexualities. These eleven stories take full advantage of that opportunity as they voyage into the futures that could await us.

THE ALYSON ALMANAC, $9.00. Almanacs have long been popular sources of information, and here at last is an almanac specifically for gay men and lesbians.

EIGHT DAYS A WEEK, by Larry Duplechan, $7.00. Can a black gay pop singer whose day starts at 11 p.m. find happiness with a white banker who's in bed by ten? This love story is one of the funniest you'll ever read.

SUPPORT YOUR LOCAL BOOKSTORE

Most of the books described above are available at your nearest gay or feminist bookstore, and many of them will be available at other bookstores. If you can't get these books locally, order by mail using this form.

- -

Enclosed is $_____ for the following books. (Add $1.00 postage when ordering just one book. If you order two or more, we'll pay the postage.)

1. _____

2. _____

3. _____

name: _____ address: _____

city: _____ state: _____ zip: _____

ALYSON PUBLICATIONS
Dept. B-95, 40 Plympton St., Boston, MA 02118

After December 31, 1992, please write for current catalog.